A Brief, Yet Concise History of Tentacular Sex

Dr. Ben Hung,

Table of Contents

Forward by the well-respected author

Being the world's foremost expert on Tentacular Sex, that is, for the layperson, sex with tentacle creatures, is not always easy. Imagine what I go through at parties, when I am asked to explain my specialty and field of study. How do you break it to a group of nuns at a charity function? And, oh, the questions I receive. Is that even physically possible? Is that illegal? Where can I find one of these pyromaniac distant octopi relatives to give me a thrill?

No, it is not always easy being an expert on such a remote subject. Although this field of study comes with a downside, it also has many benefits. I get to go to exotic locations and hunt down people who have had spectacular, Tentacular experiences and record them, ensuring that the stories are preserved for future generations. It is with determination and a straight face (even though I'm Gay) that I record every detail of these unusual tales, to the best of my ability. It is my job to ensure that the world understands the value, both historically speaking and in modern times of the many-orifice invading creatures that live in caves, under the sea and in remote jungles across the world. Even those that come from other planets, although, that is a relatively new field of study, but it is one I am willing to explore at length. The length of a tentacle.

Because of my hard work and dedication, we have uncovered many species that the world did not believe in before and contained them in zoos where we can scientifically dissect them and study their parts until they die from it. Now, if that doesn't make a man realize that he has found his calling, nothing will. Also, because of my research into the world of tentacle erotica and sexual dalliances with octo-critters, I have managed to put together an index of sorts, for librarians and historians to use as reference when suggesting Tentacular literature.

One of the questions I am asked the most often, is if I have personally shared in the joys of tentacle sex. Sadly, I must admit that I have not had the pleasure, although I have come close on a number of occasions. I hold out hope that eventually I will write an autobiography detailing my career, and that there will be a chapter in it describing my very own experiences with a tentacle monster.

One always needs hope for the future.

There are a variety of tentacle sex situations all across the world. Some have even formed meaningful relationships with tentacle monsters, and in Southern Africa, earlier this year, legislation began to ensure that one could marry a tentacle monster without prejudice. I support this, love is love, no matter how many arms and legs it has. You must enter into this field of study with an open mind, for you never know what you will encounter on your journey. I ask that you do that, when reading this book. Keep an open mind and allow the tentacles to explore you, wherever they may roam.

Thank you for taking an interest in my scientific studies. I hope that you will feel both more educated and fulfilled by the time you are finished.

Ben Hung, Ph.D., December 2016

The first recorded case of Tentacular sex

There has been some debate amongst the scientific community as well as on the many blogs and chatrooms and message boards out there about the first recorded case in history where Tentacular sex appeared. Even I, after dedicating my life to the study of this phenomenon, have been led down the wrong roads and had to do many hours of intense research to discover an original source, and prove its authenticity.

It was thought, until the mid-nineteen-eighties, that an ancient depiction discovered on the wall of a tomb in Egypt, depicting a rather famous pharaoh, Ramses II porking an octopus-like creature that descended in a chariot from the heavens, could have been the oldest record of such an event. Then, they realized after bringing in a famous Egyptologist, that it was actually considerably more recent, and proved to be a fake. It turns out a field trip from a local school had resulted in children using crayons to draw on the walls, and that their teacher, a one Mrs. Moneygrubber had allowed it, hoping to make herself rich and famous.

Egyptologists have not yet mentioned the mental state of the above noted children.

Nerō Claudius Caesar Augustus Germanicus or Emperor Nero, appears to be the first recorded case of a historical figure developing a relationship with a tentacle monster. Yes, this is the same Nero who became famous for playing his fiddle during the burning of Rome. It turns out there is a story behind that.

According to the historian Tacitus, who lived one century after the emperor, Nero was about as corrupt and untrustworthy as they came. Everything he did was to gain political advantage for himself, including when he did the tentacle monster. In 64 A.D., the Great Fire of Rome decimated most of the ancient city. Until recently, historians thought the fire was caused by Nero himself, directly, in order to clear space for his planned palace, the Domus Aurea. Although he was the first emperor to commit suicide, and probably killed both his own mother and his brother, Brittanicus, he wasn't altogether a bad guy. He had moments of tenderness, mostly with the tentacle monster. Thank goodness for accurate record keeping.

In a diary discovered many years later, written by the hand of the emperor himself, he recalled meeting the eight-legged tentacle creature in a Roman bath house. Their secret relationship developed over the course of a year or more. It was cool to be Gay, you could be a eunuch and be well respected, but tentacle sex was another matter. Although Ireland was well on the way to proving that sex with other species would not only be tolerated, but encouraged (see sheep during the potato famine on Wiki) it was still early times.

The already turbulent life of Emperor Nero could have come to an end much sooner if the people of Rome would have discovered his multi-legged lover. They carried on in secret, Nero promising Octoneptunicus, as he called the creature (meaning many talented appendages) that he would eventually flee the city and they would run away together. It seems this suited the monster, as he wanted nothing more than to be the permanent partner of the emperor.

Then things went wrong. One of the members of the Roman Council saw through a window into the bathhouse, that Nero was being pegged by the tentacle monster and blackmailed the emperor, threatening to reveal his secret if Nero did not pay up the agreed sum, which, sadly, was never recorded. Nero had no choice but to end the relationship with Octoneptunicus, which angered the monster.

The tentacle creature had a very fiery temper, literally. When he would get angered, the glands in his skin would produce a petrol-like substance and he would burst into flames from his own body heat. This did not hurt the creature at all, as it was his natural defense, but it wasn't great for anything around the monster that happened to be flammable. Which, was all of Rome.

Also, Nero's underwear. His fig leaf burst into flames and he ripped it off, throwing it into some bushes, which, then caught fire. The fire spread, and the rest, as they say, is history. Rome burnt to the ground and Nero sat diddling the tentacle monster as it did.

These are some of the dangers of tentacle-related sex acts, which, we will discuss further in a later chapter.

As you can see from the above text, tentacle monsters are not only intelligent beings, but also have strong emotional ties to those they interact with. The poet Assimus, circa 1224, once said "They have a heart for each of their appendages, which, they would wear upon their sleeves if they had any."

But, that would be hard, since their shirts would have to have eight sleeves, and that is most unusual with most clothing historically coming from sweat shops. Of course, one is lucky if a shirt has two sleeves, so, eight would be quite the unusual anomaly.

Famous examples of tentacle sex from around the globe

In 1752 one of the most infamous cases of Tentacular sex ever recorded took place off the coast of Greenland. A colossal sea beast, first thought to be a giant octopus, but later identified as "the Kraken," attacked a sailing ship full of hearty sailors. The beast first thought it would get a free meal, as it had heard that sailing vessels were yummy, from other Kraken in the immediate area. But after nearly toppling the ship with its massive tentacles, it realized there was much more fun to be had than a quick, easy meal.

Romantically inclined toward the many sailors on the ship, the Kraken had his way with each of them, leaving a few of them worse for the wear, as it is said the Kraken has spikes in the center of its giant suckers. But, sucker they did. They suckered every last member of the crew, until none of them could sail the ship and it drifted back to port twenty-nine days later, with the delirious sailors telling tales of a man-defiling beast with many tentacle legs and the strength to take down a ship.

No one believed them, and the men never worked again. Or had sex. None of them. Nightmares, the whole lot.

Different cultures have seen evidence of giant, squid or octopus-like creatures attacking sailing vessels or washing up on beaches for many centuries. Greek mythology recorded a female monster, the Scylla, which lived on the rocks of a narrow straight, and would wait for men to come along in a ship, then attack them and drag them back to her rocks. At the time, it was believed that she wanted to eat them, but now, after further research, we realize the error in such belief. She was simply searching for companionship, and a way to fill her amorous emptiness. It has to be hard being a sea monster. There aren't even any reliable dating services.

On through the annals of time, or should I say anals? There have been many recorded incidents involving many-armed beasts that have made sexual contact with human beings. Another well documented incident happened when Charlemagne, also known as Charles the Great and Charles I, had a lengthy affair with a tentacle monster during his reign as emperor. Charlemagne, as most people know, was King of the Franks. He used this title to seduce a poor and unsuspecting, and vulnerable tentacle monster who had recently lost a limb in a battle with a surviving, prehistoric shark called Megalodon.

You see, Charlemagne had somewhat of a complex. Being the oldest son of a man named "Pepin the Short," he grew up being teased about the size of his *empire*, many of the bully's in his class saying that he got the short end of the stick when it came to royalty. He felt, as an adult, that he must prove that his *lengthy* sovereignty was worthy of a King and although he naturally stood taller than Pepin, his father, he needed to be a force of brute masculinity in order to make an image for himself.

So it was, that he demanded that everyone called him "the Father of Europe," and even managed to get the Pope involved in his scheme to appear...*bigger*. Charlemagne only used his sexual prowess to engage the affections of the tentacle monster for political gain. He grew weary of fighting with the Saxons, who claimed that his policies were too entrenched in the beliefs of the left wing, so he tried to make the tentacle monster his chief advisor to the throne. He figured then, it would no longer be a matter of left wing or right wing, (or in this case, tentacle) but he could rather be left, right, top and bottom all at the same time, as well as four other cardinal directions that he could name after himself, since the charm of being called the Father of Europe was wearing off and he wanted to claim something else.

The problem came, when he approached the good citizens of Europe, promising them all these different political alliances, but then the tentacle monster, who we shall refer to as Octogenarian, could not deliver, since he was missing a limb. Those in the South, where the limb was gone, were very upset and it began a civil war among Europe.

When the tentacle monster realized he was being used, he told the secret of the great King. That he was covertly a cross-dresser and had paid to have the panties of Mary, Queen of Scots shipped to him from Ebay, (no word on what he paid) and pranced around in them singing show tunes, (which, were highly popular then) every evening after holding court. And so, came the end of Charlemagne's thirteen year reign.

It has been said that upon his death, people cried and wailed upon the sun-kissed land—or something like that, but it was the tentacle monster who wailed the loudest. The former King had destroyed his self-esteem and left him a hollow shell of the tentacle monster he was.

Please take a moment of silence in observance of the tentacle monster's pain.

Thank you.

Asia also has a long history with tentacle monsters, especially when it comes to encounters with commercial fisherman. Some people think this is a revenge tactic of the sea monsters, since if they are caught, they tend to be eaten as Sushi before they can express any love.

Warning to readers: this next section contains graphic violence against tentacle creatures, which, may produce unwanted side-effects, including sympathy and nightmares. Read at your own discretion.

A common practice throughout the centuries in Asia, has been the luring of hapless tentacle monsters to group sex parties. Always up for a good time, the poor monster and all of its tentacles will be invited by a fisherman to a party at a prestigious address, usually a sushi restaurant, where they will go to the address, packed on ice, expecting to have a good time. In the beginning, the party will meet their expectations.

After a rousing round of group sex (I will spare you the details, just use your imagination) the tentacle monster will then be subdued by much alcohol, until it is unable to protest the treatment it shall receive.

The real party will then commence. Chefs with Ginsu knives will appear from seemingly nowhere, attacking the poor creature limb by limb. Chop! Chop! Chop! The knives will hack and hack until there is nothing left of the tentacles, and then they will be wrapped in seaweed or made into soup.

These sexual sushi parties are now illegal, thanks to the tireless efforts of the "Save the Tentacle Monsters" Foundation, which, has now added tentacle creatures of all kinds to a protected wildlife list, making this practice highly illegal. Of course, this does not stop the illicit harvesting, import and consumption of the much sought-after tentacle monsters. At least they have a little fun before they die. If you must find a silver lining in something so awfully tragic.

It is not just businessmen that engage in this illegal practice. People from all walks of life are involved. The government, the everyday people and the fisherman themselves. The misunderstood tentacle creatures hardly stand a chance with so many people plotting against them all at once. It is hard to believe that so many innocent monsters could be sacrificed this way, but it is true. It happens more than you think, or more than the people involved would ever like to admit.

There is an estimated three or maybe even four tentacle monsters a year that have to go through this terrifying ordeal. There have been no known survivors to date. Which, makes you wonder how in the hell I know about it. I told you, many hours of research and first hand contact with people who are in the know. Don't worry. I will black out their faces and use voice changers for the purpose of this book, not to mention changing their names that I haven't bothered to include.

We will visit one more fascinating place before we move on to the next chapter, The United States of America, where tentacle sex is as common as apple pie. Except it is tentacle pie. Gross. I gotta try it. You know you want to.

North America, and the United States in particular is all about shock value. You need go no further than the checkout stand at the local supermarket to see valid evidence of this. The Royal Family and Michael Jackson aside, monsters, and even tentacle monsters are a hot topic. Who had sex with which creature, which politician was blackmailed, all of these have been headlines at one time or another, but, did you ever realize how many of these stories are true? Seriously, people. Read between the lines and you will find truth, even in the most outrageous tabloids. A lot of American headlines involved tentacle monsters without ever mentioning them. Watergate. Elvis. The moon landing. The evidence is often in the photos. What is that funny looking thing off in the corner of the photo that appears to have been nearly cropped out?

Tentacle.

You see scandalous photos of a celebrity wife cheating? Look in the background.

Tentacles.

Yes, the very founding of America was touched by the tentacle. After a torrid affair with a tentacle monster by the name of Betsy, John Hancock insisted she sign a certain document, causing an ink smear that looked a lot like a sucker. Because it was.

Tentacles.

We also owe a lot of great discoveries to the tentacle monsters. One particular experiment that had to do with electricity has not been reported truthfully. There was no kite and no key and no electrical storm, just a guy named Ben wading in the ocean and a tentacle monster playing with an electric eel in the shallows. How sad, that even now credit has never been given where it was due.

The very first tentacle brothel was set up in Nevada in the late 1800's. During a silver and gold boom, a lot of would be fortune seekers moved across the US to see what they could find buried in the dusty hills of Nevada. One very successful camp in Northern Nevada, which would go on to be known as Virginia City, used to be called Suckerville. This was not just because a lot of suckers moved there and then realized they were still broke years later, although that would have been a perfectly reasonable explanation for the name.

No, it was named after a certain attraction that kept the miners and fortune seekers...uh...coming. Tootsie's House of Tentacles was the star attraction in the town for many seasons. One could be guaranteed a good time there, drinking, gambling and experiencing the joys of Tentacular ladies of all kinds. Short and fat, spotted, just a few appendages or many, whatever your pleasure was, Tootsie's offered it.

It wasn't until some bozo decided that prostitution had to be legalized and controlled and that tentacle monsters would no longer be allowed in the fold that things changed. One could no longer offer up a golden nugget for tentacle services at Tootsie's. Instead, the men began to move out of the area and search for their fortunes somewhere else. If you ever want to kill an economy quickly, simply shut down the most popular business. When Tootsie's and the Tentacular staff were forced to shut down, the town did so right alongside it. So very sad.

Tootsie herself went on to become rather famous in her own right, cutting her losses and going on to a singing career that launched her into stardom. She changed her name to Aretha Franklin.

The west may have been partially won by the tentacle monster. Ever wonder why there are so few reliable photos of the famous cowboys and outlaws from the Old West?

Tentacles.

Anyway, other than that, tentacle monsters have also become popular subjects for films and movies. "50 shades of Suckers," "the King's Tentacles," "Eight Arms in a Duffel Bag," and more have been produced using the real life stories of these poor, misunderstood creatures. They have been scorned by the same society that eats them up (literally and metaphorically) at the box office and in literature, which, we will discuss further in the next chapter.

As early writers became more prolific and readers more discerning, there was a need to include more and more tentacles. A simple two or four-legged creature was no longer enough for the huge appetites of the masses. When "Tentacles and Sensibility" came out, people were not only eager to read the book and recommend it to all of their friends, but the production of tentacle memorabilia began in full force.

Who out of us can say that they do not own at least one tentacle hat? That's right. You know you have one hidden somewhere. Through the progression of time, man began thinking that he was master of the universe, and what chance did a tentacle creature have but to become part of his evil master plan? Tentacles from all different species and situations have been sold into sex work of various kinds.

From tentacle massage parlors (they only need one employee) to websites promising hot tentacle action, these mistreated monsters have been used and abused by those who are looking to make a quick buck, tentacle over fist.

If you know a monster that has been sold into sex work, the kindest thing you can do is kill it and stop the illegal profit ring. I would tell you to call a number and report it, but these are tentacle monsters, not pandas or other endangered wildlife, and they aren't cute like puppies, so therefore there is no hotline and no one really gives a crap. Except you, because you are taking the time to read about these unfortunate events and be empathetic to the cause. You could also make signs for your front yard that say something to the effect of "Tentacles have rights! Free the Monsters!" I'd be cool with that, as long as the sign is on your lawn and not mine.

You can now see what I mean, when I say that the reach of tentacles is farther than we once thought. At least 5 feet in most cases. Some even longer than that. Very useful when you are hanging out with a tentacle monster on the couch and you can't reach the remote or the beer cooler.

In one now infamous case, a robber walked into a liquor store in New York, pointed a gun at the cashier and demanded everything in the register. When the cashier handed over the money, the robber shot him in the arm anyway to slow his reaction time. When he reached the doors of the store though, trying to make his great escape, a tentacle monster was waiting for him. The monster wrapped his arms around the guy and detained him until cops could arrive, using his free arms to administer first aid to the cashier and buy and pay for a round of beers for the police.

Misunderstanding the situation, the cops thought that the monster was the robber and attacked him with brutal force. It took three years for all of the tentacle monster's arms to grow back and he successfully sued the State of New York for police brutality. He was awarded eight million dollars, that's one million for each arm he lost. It was close though, since the officers tried to use the defense that the tentacle monster had been "armed." He proved that he wasn't by the time they were finished with him.

As you can see, not all monsters are bad, and some of them can actually be heroes. It is unfair to judge them all the same way and stereotype them just for having more arms than we do.

Tentacles in Literature

As we briefly discussed earlier, there have been a lot of famous cases of tentacles in literature. One may not even realize how many until someone takes the time to properly compile a list, which, I will not do because A.) I am too lazy and B.) I'm already working on my next terrible book and don't have time. This stuff takes some serious research.

What I will do, is list some of the better titles that deal with tentacle monsters here, so that you may look them up and enjoy them as you please. Many of these are classic titles that are free in the public domain, or a nearby trash receptacle. Whichever is easier for you to get to.

Here are some titles for you to check out:

Tentacles in 1984

The Adventures of Tentacleberry Fins

Lolita and the Octopus

The sound and the Fury of the Kraken

The Tentacled Catcher in the Rye

Tentacle's Travels

A Brave New Monster

The Divine Comedy of Eight Arms

Lord of the Suckers

Wuthering Tentacles (A Seaman's Tale)

Call of the Octopoid

Frankententacle

Tentacles in Wonderland

The Suckers also Rise

The Scarlett Tentacle

Limbs and Punishment (A 50 Shades Prequel)

A Farewell to Arms (Autobiography of that Poor Monster at the Liquor Shop in New York.)

Counting the Arms of Monte Cristo

Great Expectations of Sea Monsters

The Old Man and the Sea Monster

The Strange Case of Dr. Jekyll and Mr. Likes to Hyde (things with his tentacles)

Count them Dracula

A Tale of Two Monsters

Interview with the Tentacle Vampire

20,000 Leagues Under the Sea is My sex Cave

The Thirteen Armed Musketeers

Around the World in Eighty Arms

A Midsummer Night's Tentacle Orgy

And of course, no list would be complete without

Tentacle Twist (sounds painful but some people dig that.)

There are also a number of popular books that are not classics, but who wants to read those when you have to pay for them? I will mention a few anyway.

Gone Octopi

Harry Sucker and the Giblets of Fur

The Girl on the Tentacle

When Breath Becomes Air Bubbles

Go Set a Tentacle

All the Ink we cannot Pee

Obviously this is just a few of the many jewels you can find hidden amongst the other titles at your local library. Good luck finding them online, as most retailers seem to have a thing for banning all the most historically important tentacle literature.

So, what, you may ask is the deal with the tentacle censorship? Well, I have no fucking clue.

Next chapter.

Mistaken Identity: Objects not Tentacular

Ever hear those stories where someone finds a suspicious package and they close down an entire city block to deal with it, only to find out it was a burger in a paper bag? This misidentification happens quite regularly in the case of tentacle monsters. Not that they all turn out to be burgers. That only happens in the Southern US.

In any case, there have been many cases, especially in more recent years, where people reported seeing strange monsters of all varieties, including those that are not of the tentacle type that just turned out to be animals, or other objects, nothing mysterious at all. Not to say that there have been no actual sightings or encounters with tentacle creatures, because that would be a BOLD FACED LIE. But there have been some serious cases of misidentification. In the examples that follow, people have been convinced they saw a tentacle monster, only to find out that was not the case through later discovery.

One case happened on the morning of July 9th, 1981 in the swamps of Monroe, Arkansas. A rather quiet swamp by most standards, full of the usual array of birds, hunting blinds and hillbilly families, the swamp was most suddenly disturbed by the sound of gunshots and an old 4X4 vehicle as well as the swearing and screaming of a group of duck hunters that decided to give chase to an unknown species they believed they saw emerging from the swamp.

"It's terrible," one witness said, with her hair still in curlers. She would have said more, but the interview ended. You can tell, however, from her intense interview, that it must have been a very bad experience. Huh, even that sentence was longer than her interview.

Anyway, one of the hunters believed that he saw a snakelike arm come out of the swamp and begin searching the land. Figuring he could bag a snake and use it as a hatband while he waited for the ducks to appear, he took a pot shot at the creature, only to realize that there were more of them than he thought.

"There was hundreds," he later told the media, swearing that it was not a fish story. "The thing was goin' to eat us, but then I shot it and scared it away. There's something livin' in that swamp. Something we all better watch out fer."

This, of course, caused a sensation in Monroe, and soon the entire local squadron of hillbillies arrived toting guns and pitchforks and torches and all organized into the usual disorganized mob mentality, all clamoring to be the first to bag the 'Beast of Monroe.'

Two guys shot each other on accident. One guy took a pitchfork to the head, but it was over an unrelated matter, and one woman swore she saw the beast trying to drag her bean and possum casserole from her oven and into the swamp. No one believed that anyone got shot, but there was an uproar over the potential theft of the homemade casserole. You just don't invade a good woman's kitchen and steal the food for her family. You just don't. No respectable swamp monster would ever do that.

They searched the swamps in teams for weeks, but came up empty handed. It was assumed that the beast had moved on and eventually the hullabaloo began to die down, the hillbillies' interests returning to normal matters for the area, like beer and ducks.

That is, until one day, when a younger hillbilly, Bubba-Jo, went for a hike out in swamps, planning to bag a gator for his girlfriend. He had only been out there for a number of minutes, when he felt the hair on the back of his neck stand on end, and he looked to his left, where a very long, snakelike arm slithered through the trees and right at him.

He raised his shotgun and fired off two rounds, but the creature did not react. Curious as to how it could be hit with a direct shot and not feel it, he moved closer. Upon inspection, he realized that the famed Beast of Monroe, was none other than some plastic tubing that the local branch of the EPA had been using to conduct studies on pollution of ground water.

He still took a selfie with it, even cutting off a chunk to take home to his girlfriend in lieu of the gator tail he had originally intended to get for her. One would think, that this would have embarrassed the hillbillies, but they still swear the item was unrelated to their original discovery.

"It's still out there," the lead hillbilly said in a later interview.

I guess we will never know for sure...

There have been many cases of mistaken tentacle identification in water sources, from the ocean, to lakes, rivers and streams around the world. Usually, these end up being logs, fishing decoys or other items floating in the water that when glimpsed from a distance, appear to be a foreign creature of some type. This kind of misunderstanding has been happening for many centuries, but people never learn from history and so, idiots keep reporting seeing monsters that aren't really there.

There was a recent report in India that a giant tentacled monster emerged from a toilet and felt up the user. It turned out it was really a boa constrictor, matter solved. At least it made the guy feel safe again about using the toilet when it turned out it was only a giant, man eating snake rather than some unidentified cryptid.

There have even been reports of enormous, tentacle monsters in the New York City Sewer systems, that upon closer inspection, simply turned out to be pet octopi that people had flushed down the toilet. They didn't mutate like sewer turtles or gators have been known to do, they simply grew to their normal size, but in the dark and cold and smelly chambers of the sewer system, employees of the city seemed to think they were ten times the size they actually were. I can relate. Sometimes, in the middle of the night, the stapler on my desk takes on an ominous quality, appearing large and hungry with demented staple fangs that appear to have blood dripping from them. Simple cases of mistaken identity.

A lot of reports seem to come from Scotland. Perhaps it is the volatile history of the loch, but Nessie seems to have set the mood for the country. Now, this would make more sense if the Scottish folk were well known for their consumption of alcohol, but we all know that isn't the case. Clearly, the English are the drunks of Britain as a whole. We aren't mentioning the Welsh, because they are barely even

British, and only by default are they connected to the tri-country area known as Britain in the first place.

Oh, those Scots. Every year, thousands of reports of strange occurrences, from lights in the sky, to sea monsters, to tentacle monsters stealing kilts and bagpipes, come flooding in to the local authorities. One Scotsman, during a walk home with his sheep from a local pub, swore that a Tentacular creature attacked him, stealing the last of his available cash and holding him at tentacle point, causing him to lose his herd of sheep and his kilt. It turned out, he was so stone cold drunk (so much for that) that he had run into a tree, fought with the drooping branches of the weeping willow, bellowing in fear and the sheep had run off in terror. His kilt was later found hanging in said tree, torn to shreds.

When one of the flock of sheep was interviewed, he said, "Baah. Terrifying."

Another lengthy interview that I have included in this book for the purpose of verification. You can see that I have made every effort to be authentic wherever possible. I wouldn't want you to doubt the intention of this author.

Another reported incident in Scotland is quite historical. A Scotsman by the name of Braveheart led his people to victory over oppression, or so history tells it. In reality, it was just Braveheart, some guy that left a sporting event with a face half-painted blue, and sixteen tentacle monsters that won the battle. From a distance though, because of the many arms of the sixteen freedom fighters, it looked like there were many soldiers and the Enquirer, the most important news rag of the period reported it all incorrectly. So, in this case, you can clearly see that the tentacle monsters were once again denied their proper glory through misidentification. Poor bastards just can't catch a break.

When things wash up on beaches and are not identified as any known animal, the cryptozoologists are called in to perform testing and try to identify the creatures. When things are not as simple as a misidentified bundle of seaweed, it can get really confusing. Think, Montauk Monster. For weeks people believed that they had discovered some strange hybrid species created by the government, but it turned out to be a raccoon.

The Bayside Beast was much the same. Something washed ashore in Bayside California that those who found it could not identify, a rather large something. It turned out to be a giant squid, and although that was slightly frightening in and of itself, it was not a creature unknown to science and didn't make the people rich as they were hoping to become from the discovery.

There have also been a lot of hoaxes over the years that have made the science of cryptozoology more of a minefield and less of a respected profession. People have used every conceivable combination of items, including hoses, tires, gelatinous substances and even their grandmother's underwear to try and create creatures that appeared real enough to fool the public. It tends to come unraveled (the story not the panties) when they are asked to provide the specimen they supposedly found for scientific study. Either the carcass comes up missing, or they do not wish to donate their find to science. Usually, at some point one of the original group who made the great discovery ends up admitting it was a hoax and blaming the entire thing on one of the others in the group.

So, the important lesson to learn from this chapter, is that everything you see that looks suspicious may not be an actual tentacle monster, although it is not impossible that you will eventually see one. If you do encounter the corpse of a tentacle beast, be sure to notate everything about the area as if you were processing a crime scene. Take notes, take photos and ensure that you take particularly clear selfies with the beast so you can post them to social media and show off to your friends.

If you decide to donate the body to science, and if, in fact, it is still there when you get to the spot where it lie with the science team, ensure that you have named the cryptoid after yourself and copyrighted it so that no one else can claim the discovery. Then try selling your photos to a well-respected junk tabloid. You might make yourself a few bucks and get a few rounds on the house the next time you go to a local bar.

The possible dangers of Tentacular sex

Not to say that there is anything wrong with having a tentacle fetish, or even a tentacaculaphilia, but there are some things that you should keep in mind. This chapter is devoted entirely to warning you about unsafe Tentacular sex and how to avoid putting yourself into situations where you may find yourself overwhelmed by the sheer number of appendages you will be dealing with if such a thing is to occur.

Everyone who goes into tentacle sexual situations in this century is far more aware of the dangers than those were in the past. Poor Nero. We now understand that the danger of having giant sucker marks all over your body after such an encounter is present and that you may need a lot of makeup and time off of work to cover up your private activities.

This is not the only danger.

It has often been said that mothers could use more arms than they are blessed with. In the case of tentacle creatures, both male and female, this is not true. They often find that the number of appendages they have get in the way when trying to perform even the simplest of tasks, such as making coffee, or using a riding crop on their intended lover.

It is always a good idea to have a safe word when dealing with Tentacular creatures, as they can become frustrated with their own limbs not cooperating and take it out on their intended partner. I recommend using the word "sushi," as it is both something that usually does not come up during sex and is also a brutal reminder to your Tentacular partner of what can become of them if they misbehave. This may sound harsh, but you must remain in control at all times when you have only half the number of limbs, if not less, than your partner.

We briefly discussed the flaming tentacle creature when we talked about the burning of Rome. If you notice that your potential partner smells of brimstone, tends to flare up red when they get angry or excited, or releases random puffs of thick, black smoke, it might be a good idea to show up to your liaison dressed in firefighter's garb and carry a fire extinguisher, a hose, or both. If this is not possible, then keep a blanket nearby to throw over the flaming critter should the unthinkable happen. Fires caused by arsonist crypto creatures are taken much more seriously by law enforcement now than they were during early civilization.

There are also electrical tentacle creatures, mind-controlling tentacle creatures and space invader tentacle creatures who only wish to probe and discover the secrets of their lovers, so unless that is your thing, you should be wary.

As there are no legitimate sites out there to check out the background of your potential tentacle lover, you will have to rely on good judgment when you meet to decide if it is safe to proceed with them or if they are likely to squeeze the life out of you and then suck your brain through your nose cavity. Of course, the likelihood that you will lose much brain if you are the type that is going to have sex with a tentacle monster is so remote anyway that you probably won't be losing much, in fact, you may not even notice. Just saying.

Regardless, you should always be careful. Never meet your tentacle partner in a dark alley, or in a place where there is no cell reception. You should meet in a well-lit area where you will expose yourself to the scrutiny of the masses for your first date. It might be awkward, but at least it will give you the chance to assess the character of said monster.

Once this has happened and you have had a chance to size up your monster, if you choose to take it further and go home with them, wherever that may be, to your home or theirs, it is important to lay down ground rules. Which orifices are off limits, how many tentacles can be stuck in each one and whether you are comfortable with squeeze play, since tentacles tend to have a mind of their own must be set out clearly and defined before engaging in actual foreplay. Things tend to move rapidly with tentacle monsters, them not always being the most romantic of cuddlers.

After you have laid down the ground rules and agreed to a safe word, you should be ready to begin. Please read the next chapter for tips on how to seduce your tentacle monster.

A guide to Tentacular seduction

Okay, so you have gotten this far and now you understand the fascinating history of Tentacular sex as well as some of the possible dangers of engaging in such acts. You are cool with the sucker marks and all other hazards and have decided to go for it. Now you must find yourself a potential tentacled lover to complete your fantasy. But where do you find them and what do you do to approach them once you have located one? Have no fears that is what this chapter is all about.

Whereas you might pick up a random tentacle monster in a seedy section of town while you are bar-hopping on a random Saturday night, it is not likely. Besides, many of these monsters have been sold into prostitution and that is not always a safe choice for a partner. They can have diseases that can be spread to humans, such a suckerlococcis and tentacle herpes. No, you want to steer clear of those sorts and go for a purer monster to fill your sexual and emotional needs.

Where are you likely to encounter this type of creature? Look back into history for some clues. Where do Hercules and Hobbits fight hydras and other such beasts? In lakes. So, if you are thinking of taking a weekend away to visit a lake and do some "fishing" (wink wink) then you should do the following:

Learn where the lake monster has been recently sighted. Usually they live in the depths, but they like to visit the surface to see what's going on from time to time. Make yourself smell as much like a fish as possible. It will lure them to you. I recommend rolling in chum. When you smell like shark bait, you will have succeeded in task one.

Once you have made yourself smell appealing to the monster, then you should try making some mating calls. These are squishy, sticky, sucking sounds like when you walk around in wet tennis shoes. So, naturally that is what you should do. Don't be afraid to get your feet wet. Jump right in and wet those tennies down, socks and all and then walk around the area, making sucking noises from your feet.

Step three is the hardest of the bunch. Once you have gotten the attention of the tentacle monster, you must encourage them to come closer to you and form a bond of trust. The best way to do this, is to wine and dine them from the shore. You can lay out squid, octopus or other smaller tentacles creatures to lure them onto the beach, and then offer them a nice glass of beer or wine, depending on the likes and dislikes of your potential date. Some sea monsters and lake monsters are more refined than others. They also have a thing for cheese, and the stinkier it is, the better. If you can manage to capture the attention of the monster and hold it, you are halfway there.

The next step is to bat your eyes and show a little skin. The idea of the tentacles wrapping around your body may excite you, but it also excites the monster. They love the idea of being able to mark you as their own with their circular suckers and to own you in demented ways that only a multi-armed monster could. Once you have them where you want them that is on the beach or wherever you have located one, you will be able to begin wooing them with your sexual prowess, nearly the same as you would a human partner. Tentacle monsters like flowers, chocolates and to be told they are beautiful, or handsome, depending on the sex of the monsters.

Compliment them frequently and share things about yourself so that they feel more comfortable. If you have been a fan of tentacles your entire life, share that information with them. It will make your initial bond stronger. You can also ask them to talk about themselves. What depth do they live at, how many sailors and swimmers have they eaten in the past, are they into open relationships, are they related to the kraken. You know, the usual first date fare. While you don't want to get too personal right away, you want them to feel comfortable and like they can talk to you about anything. If language is a barrier, try signing. They have a lot of arms and can carry on a conversation in sign language very adequately.

Once you have lured your tentacle monster from the water, what to do next is up to you. If you choose to follow my advice (my attorney says to tell you this is never recommended and even less practiced) then take your Tentacular future soul mate to a public park and get to know them better. Or just go to the nearest cave and get it on. I will not explain to you how to have tentacle sex in the briefest and least provocative fashion that I can to avoid censorship from the publishing gods.

1. Go to the cave or other hideout of the monster
2. Keep in mind this is better because you can't breathe underwater
3. Set ground (or aerial depending on intent) rules
4. Continue making sucking sounds to create ambience
5. Embrace monster and compliment tentacles

6. Expose yourself to the monster and let him/her explore you

7. Make happy noises to show appreciation

8. Relax into the embrace of the tentacles

9. Kiss and gently encourage the monster (this will be slimy or bumpy or both)

10. Give in to your desires and offer up all agreed upon orifices.

11. Have a wild, sultry time

12. Explain to monster that you can only meet in secret until the laws change

13. Write a biography and publish it

14. Make money

If you live to tell about it, then you have accomplished your mission and you will be able to write that account and make money from it. If not, then at least you had a good time. Either way, I am not to be held responsible for any failures to stay alive.

Afterward

I hope that this book has helped explain the important rules of tentacles in our modern society, as well as their importance throughout history. I want all who read this book to come...away, feeling like they have been well-informed and learned things that they did not know before.

I have done my best to offer you unique information that you will not find published in other books on this subject, if you are ever unlucky enough to cross another book on this subject, that is.

It is our responsibility as human beings to obtain knowledge and make records of it for the benefit of future generations, and that was my goal when writing this book. If you have had a tentacle experience and wish to share it, please write your own book, so mine does not look so lonely in this unique and remote category.

As I sit here this evening at my desk, staring out the window and writing the last little bit of this important and educational nonfiction book, I am reminded that I have come a long way from my humble beginnings. It would not have been possible to write this book without the help of absolutely no one, because no one wanted to be asked questions about tentacle sex, regardless of what I may have alluded to in the beginning of the book. Small oversight.

Anyhow, as I sit here writing the closing for this book I am left with the odd sensation of something creeping up my leg...and to my...

"Oh! What is that? That looks quite Tentacular, indeed!"

As I write this afterward.

"Oh! Right there...that's good. Keep doing that with that fourth tentacle...oh yeah...mmmmm."

Screw the afterward.

"Here monster, monster, monster, daddy wants to play."

Author of Weird Books Found Dead in Home Office with

Sucker Marks from Attacker

A white, thirty-something author was found dead yesterday at his humble home. He was still seated in front of his computer, and evidence suggests that he was attacked by some kind of tentacled beast that he invited over after responding to a singles listing in a local paper and responding to it. Single, purple and white tentacle monster seeks companion for romantic purposes. The ad was still on his desk among the other clutter.

The perpetrator is still on the loose according to local authorities and should be considered "very armed" and dangerous.

If you have any information about this crime, please call the hotline 1-555-beast-crimes. We guarantee that your identity will be protected and you may receive a reward if your call leads to the apprehension of the suspect.

Mr. Ben Hung passed away with a smile on his face and is survived by his cactus plant and the dust bunnies under his bed. A donation fund has been set up in his name and all proceeds will go to the maintenance of those he left behind. Thank you.

If you enjoyed this book check out the author's other books on Amazon below:

Robotic Aliens Who like Wearing Women's Underwear

Investigating the Strange Series

Elvis Really is an Alien and he helped a Toaster Pastry Seduce Me: A Really Erotic Book of Eroticness

The Trees in the Forest had Wood and it was all for Me

The Haunting of Boner Farm

The Bog Beast of Bellingham

Napoleon's Boner-Party: Or, the Day the French Ghost Gave me the Bird

Odd Critters Series

I kissed a Gay Half-Alpaca-Half-Octopus Alien from Mars and I Liked it

Printed in Great Britain
by Amazon

OVERC

BIPOLAR

DISORDER

DEFYING THE ODDS

Romain U. DuFour, III

ISBN 978-1-63630-697-1 (Paperback)
ISBN 978-1-63630-698-8 (Digital)

Covenant Books, Inc.
11661 Hwy 707
Murrells Inlet, SC 29576
www.covenantbooks.com

CONTENTS

CHAPTER 1

Diagnosis Is Not a Death Sentence

Bipolar disorder is a serious psychiatric condition. An individual who experiences this illness may experience two extremes. One extreme is mania, while the other extreme is depression. Mania is when an individual will experience a mood of great euphoria, while the depressed mood is when someone has a significant mood of deep sadness.

In previous decades, the condition was referred to as manic depression. Bipolar disorder is more prominent than ever. It is a condition that does not discriminate. Individuals from all walks of life can suffer from it.

I was initially diagnosed with this illness back in 1993. At that time, it seemed as though there were not many who were bearers of the illness. Today, it is an illness that affects millions. Now there is more support for many with the condition than ever before.

Some who are bearers of bipolar disorder in previous years might have suffered in silence. Unfortunately, society in previous years did not support many individuals with mental illness. It was considered taboo to have bipolar disorder in years past because of the ignorance and fear of those who were not affected by it. In this present time, research and knowledge of the illness has improved dramatically and significantly.

The depressive individual might have been considered strange decades ago. Sometimes an individual who was affected by the disorder was ostracized by society. When an individual was diagnosed with bipolar disorder, it seemed as though there was not any hope. The good news today is that the illness does not have to be a death sentence.

With therapy and various psychiatric medications, bipolar disorder can be monitored and treated. The bearer must not allow his or her self to have self-pity because having self-pity allows the illness to gain victory and prominence. Though bipolar disorder has a lot to do with cognitive thoughts, it is imperative that the individual, who is living and coping with the illness, tackles the condition with vigor and confidence.

This is why it is important that individuals who are diagnosed with bipolar disorder have a great support system. If an individual has at least one supportive friend or family member, it can help the individual combat the condition. Those with supportive friends and loved ones can develop hope.

When I was diagnosed with the illness over twenty-five years ago, I did not foresee living a life of success. Sure, there were times in which I struggled with the effects of this disorder. I lost friendships and relationships as a result of this condition. Faith in God and myself helped me not to become significantly overwhelmed by the symptoms of this mental illness.

Bipolar disorder is not like other illnesses and sicknesses. The illness can become unpredictable. It does not have to defeat the depressive person. Although there is no cure for the condition, one can overcome it by one's positive outlook on life.

In some instances, bipolar disorder is frowned upon. Though it is an illness that is gaining more acceptance, there is still a negative stigma that is associated with having it. Some consider those who are affected by a mental illness as being "second-class citizens." Individuals with this mindset are sadly mistaken.

I believe that there is an enormous amount of individuals in this society, who knows someone or knows of an individual with bipolar disorder or some type of mental illness. This is why the illness is gaining more popularity among the mainstream. Fortunately, there is more empathy toward bearers of the disease.

Personally, I experienced backlash from having the illness when I dated this one young lady in particular. The backlash that I received from having this disorder did not come from the woman I dated. It came from her family. There was an instance in which I was experiencing a manic episode.

During this time, I did not recognize the triggers of the illness. I must admit that I went off my medication without consulting my doctor. This was a huge mistake on my part, which resulted in behaviors that I did not normally engage in. Although this occurred over twenty years ago, I can recall how I was rambling and not being my normal self because I did want to take medicine.

As a result of my actions, my former girlfriend's family did not understand the symptoms of my illness. They did not understand the chemical imbalance that was in my brain, which resulted in my rambling. Also, lack of an adequate amount of rest compounded and escalated my condition. I was not educated enough about the disorder at that time because I was recently diagnosed with it.

After this particular episode, my former girlfriend's family forced her to end the relationship. In hindsight, I can understand why her parents told her to break up with me because during that time, mental illness and bipolar disorder were difficult to comprehend for some in society in the 1990s. Knowledge of the disorder was not as widely known back then as it is currently.

Shame was associated with individuals who were diagnosed with a mental illness. Because of lack of knowledge and empathy toward individuals with mental illness, many chose to turn their backs on those experiencing psychological disorders. Sadly, there are some who must deal with their illness on their own.

Significant strides have been made by society in regard to hospitals and organizations that specialize in the support of mental conditions. It is no longer shameful to have a psychological illness. Those who seek help for mental illness can be viewed as courageous.

If you are suffering from a psychological condition, do not allow others to frown upon you. Those that have mental illness are just as vital to society as nonbearers. As long as the depressive person is a law-abiding member of society, then respect must be given.

There are numerous ailments and illnesses that plague a significant amount of individuals in our society. It is imperative that those who are diagnosed with a serious illness do all that they can to combat it. If one is diagnosed with bipolar disorder, one must not journey through life defeated.

In previous years, it was thought that a depressive person could not dramatically improve. This is why many thought that once an individual was diagnosed with a mental illness, that individual's life was over.

After my initial diagnosis, I thought that I could not resume in my regular activities. I did not think that I could enjoy life again. Blindly and naively, I thought that partying and drinking alcohol was all there was to life.

Those who are diagnosed with mental illness must make a lifestyle change in order to gain victory over the disease. This means that the sufferer should avoid living recklessly by drinking and using other substances. I believe that an individual can make their illness worse by engaging in the use of alcohol and other chemicals.

No one who is diagnosed with a mental illness such as bipolar disorder can overcome it without a viable support system. It is imperative that the bearer has a positive relationship with friends and loved ones, as well as one's physician or therapist.

The depressive person, physician, and loved ones must work as a team. Hopefully, the bearer of the illness, the doctor, and loved one(s) can build trust amongst one another. If the bearer feels like his or her physician has their best interest, then progress can be made regarding the improvement of the individual's condition.

An individual who is diagnosed with the disorder may have a long road ahead of them. It is an illness that requires a plethora of patience. Sometimes there are various medications that a physician might try in order to reduce the symptoms of the disease. This is why the patient/doctor relationship is crucial.

An individual can live a long and prosperous life with bipolar disorder. If the bearer is going through a trying time because of this illness, I believe that the trying time will subside. Those with the disorder must acquire patience with the doctor, the medicine, and themselves.

In my opinion, bipolar disorder is an illness that is won when the depressive person has the right kind of support. I am thankful and grateful that my mother did not give up on me when I was at my worse. Because my mother prayed and had faith that my condition would improve, I was able to achieve many of my dreams and goals.

I understand that it might be difficult to have patience with a friend or loved one who is dealing with the illness. The key for me getting better was having the vision that my life would return to some sense of normalcy. Never abandon the fact that you can overcome this disorder with support from those closest to you.

In this society, there are many individuals who seek to put a label on those who are mentally ill. Some consider individuals who suffer from psychiatric conditions as eccentric. No one deserves to be a victim of a stereotype. Individuals with psychiatric disorders are not the disorder that they suffer from.

For example, an individual who suffers from heart disease or diabetes does not encounter the same type of scrutiny as those who have other medical conditions, such as bipolar disorder. Cardiovascular diseases, as well as other illnesses, affect specific areas of the body. In regard to mental illness, it affects the brain.

The goal that every human should strive for is wholeness. If an individual has an illness that ails one part of one's body, then that individual will most likely receive treatment from a physician who specializes in that specific health condition. Mental illness happens to occur in the mind.

We all need our mind and brain to make sound cognitive decisions throughout the day. One's brain is just as vital as any other area of the body. This is why it is imperative that one does not take one's mental health for granted.

Today, I am thankful that there are more outlets and support for individuals with mental disorders. Society as a whole is considering how imperative it is for an individual to be in a healthy mental state.

I can recall how I had little to no regard for my mental state when I was a teenager. It took years of coping with bipolar disorder to realize the importance of my cognitive health. Cognitive health is beneficial to one's overall wholeness and wellness.

One's mind and brain can either make or break an individual. It matters how one views oneself in one's thoughts. If your mind and thoughts are telling you that you will not improve from your mental illness, then you have inadvertently defined yourself.

The worst thing that a bearer of a mental illness can do is to accept what others' opinions are of you. Just because one might be diagnosed with a mental illness, it does not mean that one has to allow others' definition of you to define who you are. There was an encounter that I had with a former doctor who tried to define me.

I vividly remember how she told me while I was in session with her, "You know you are bipolar." It surprised me that a doctor would blatantly remind me of my disorder when I was sharing my own personal experiences. After this doctor tried to define my worth as an individual who happens to have an illness called bipolar disorder, I told her that this illness does not define my character as a person.

I must say that she was offended when I expressed to her that she was a doctor, and that is her occupation. Also, I told her that her occupation as a doctor is something that she does to make a living, and that being a doctor does not define her character, whether good or bad. I do not suggest that every depressive person remind their doctor or therapist of how not to define them, but every individual with a mental disorder must be treated with dignity and respect.

When an individual is diagnosed with any type of illness, it can become devastating news. In fact, being diagnosed with any health condition can become life changing. Those who are diagnosed with a mental disorder are no exception.

I can recall how I felt when my former doctor diagnosed me with bipolar disorder. Initially, I was relieved because there was a name given to the feelings that I felt from within. After my diagnosis, I went through a period of self-denial.

There were times that I felt that I could not accept the fact that I suffered from a mental illness. I naively thought that it was a sign of weakness to admit to others that I had a psychological disorder. It took years of self-reflection to admit to myself that I have a mental illness.

Before I was clinically diagnosed with bipolar disorder, I lived a normal and active lifestyle. I was thriving in school all throughout my formative years. Also, I was a relatively joyous person.

Life for me during the majority of my early to middle adolescence was, for the most part, enjoyable. I did not have a specific clique in school that I identified with. I knew the individuals who were members of the popular clique, as well as the individuals who were not so popular.

Because I played sports and thrived academically, I had various types of friends. During my time in elementary through high school, I believe that one could perhaps consider me well-rounded. My mood was consistent. So when I was diagnosed with a mental disorder at nineteen years of age, I was definitely shocked and surprised.

I thought that I would never become mentally ill because I lived the majority of my life, before my diagnosis, without any symptoms of a psychiatric disorder. This was why it was difficult to accept that I had a mental illness. My friends at the time of my diagnosis also could not accept the diagnosis.

Bipolar disorder or any other mental illness is not easy to accept especially by loved ones and friends. Once acceptance is established, then the bearer can also accept his or her condition. In regard to acceptance of an individual with a mental illness, hopefully, time and patience will become a determining factor.

If one is experiencing bipolar disorder or any other mental condition, it is imperative that the individual learn how to accept the diagnosis, while remaining optimistic. There are other conditions that might have a negative prognosis. The faster the individual can accept their condition, the greater the chances are that the individual can combat the disorder proactively.

In my own life, I had to learn how to accept all that encompasses being a sufferer of bipolar disorder. Also, I learned that denial could become the antithesis of growth and acceptance. An optimistic attitude can go a long way in the acceptance of combating any illness, let alone a mental disorder.

There are many things in this life that can overwhelm someone. One has to be careful not to allow bipolar disorder or any other illness to consume one's life. I believe that sufferers of mental illness are more than the disorder itself.

As an individual with mental illness, I refuse to succumb to labels. Bipolar disorder just happens to be a disease in which I suffer from, but it does not have anything to do with my character. Those who know me personally know that I am a kind and humble individual.

I believe that there are kindhearted people who just happen to have mental illness. In some cases, family genetics have contributed to an individual who might be a bearer of a psychological disorder. It is through no fault of the individuals who have a chemical imbalance that they have a psychological condition.

No one can pick and choose the family that they were born into. Personally, mental illness runs on both of my parents' sides of the family. Because mental illness in previous years was associated with both guilt and shame, the majority of my family members shied away from conversing about it.

When my mother revealed to other members of our family that I suffered from bipolar disorder, it took a plethora of courage. Some of my family members I do not have a relationship with because of the disorder. This is the chance that one takes when revealing a mental illness to others. Unfortunately, there are some with empathy, while there are others who do not have any type of sincerity.

Individuals with mental illness will be labeled by society. Many family members ostracize other family members for having a mental condition. It is as if the family member with the psychological disorder chose to have the illness.

I am certain that no one would like to be labeled for having an illness that one does not have any control over. Individuals with mental disorders must be assured that they are not what others label as *crazy*. The goal that every bearer of mental illness should strive for is self-love. Individuals with bipolar disorder and other mental illnesses cannot do anything about how society views them. Those who label others in a negative way are the individuals who are small-minded. The only way that a bearer of any mental disorder can combat small-minded individuals who label others is by proving those negative individuals wrong.

How does an individual with a mental condition prove others wrong? It is by living a prosperous and successful life. Many who have mental conditions often limit themselves. Due to the labeling of nonempathetic individuals, many who happen to have a mental condition dare to dream.

I hope that those who are depressive persons strive to keep pressing on. In this life, there is an enormous amount of achievements that one can accomplish. Remember to never allow others to write the story of your life without consulting you initially.

I must admit that there was a time that I questioned my ability to accomplish goals that I set. My confidence wavered because this illness was getting the best of me. There were times in which I fell into a deep-rooted depression.

The depression that I experienced left me in a state of utter sadness. At the time, I was extremely lethargic. I did not want to do anything but sleep. Also, I lost interest in many of the activities that I enjoyed.

It was as though the sunny days outside was filled with cloudiness. There were times that even good news did not positively influence my state of depression. I thought that I would not return to a life of consistency and happiness.

During the time in which I experienced the haze of depression, I did not foresee accomplishing my goal of graduating from college. The deep depression that I experienced lasted approximately four years. I can relate and understand how an individual with bipolar disorder can give up on life.

Some may experience the nonmanic spectrum of the illness, which is a mood of extreme sadness. If an individual is in this state, it is a great task just to get out of bed in the morning. A bearer's outlook on life becomes filled with continuous hopelessness.

If one is filled with hopelessness, then there is little to no chance that the sufferer will accomplish their goals. I believe that the individual with the disorder must restore one's vision in life. Sure, friends and loved ones can assist in restoring hope, but it starts with the individual desiring to get out of the depressed funk.

What we tell ourselves internally can make a world of difference. Positive affirmation along with support and therapy can gradually lift the mood of the depressed person. The individual with bipolar disorder can accomplish many goals.

Before the individual with the disorder can accomplish any goal, the first goal should be to establish a consistent mental state. There is no need for an individual with bipolar disorder to set lofty goals when the individual's mental state is not certain. The key to accomplishing various goals in life is by setting each goal one step at a time.

Setting minute goals one step at a time has yielded the accomplishment of various goals that I set in life. I can recall how I made up my mind initially that I would overcome my depressed state. Also, I developed a vision for my life that I would do everything in my power to improve my condition.

Once I achieved my goal of consistently remaining in a non-depressed mood, I commenced to accomplish other achievements. After I completed my goal of graduating from college, my confidence increased. Although I took a significant amount of time off from college, when I returned, I made the dean's list with straight As one semester.

This achievement was one of the goals I set for that particular semester. I realized that there are infinite possibilities I can accomplish despite having this disease. Achievements and accomplishments can be obtained, but it commences with the goal of overcoming the various moods of the illness.

In regard to an individual experiencing bipolar disorder, there is hope that the individual can overcome it. Previously, I discussed how it is imperative that the individual with the illness receives the proper support and treatment. Without sufficient support, the disorder can have precedence over the bearer's life.

I am thankful that my mother does not treat me differently because of my illness. Some who are diagnosed with bipolar disorder are sometimes pitied. Those who are closest to the individual, such as family members and friends, hinder the individual's progress by treating them with pity.

As a result of an individual being pitied, it can lead to the depressive person having self-pity. Those that have mental illness must be treated with normalcy. If the bearer of the condition is treated with normalcy, then the individual has a greater chance of overcoming the condition.

Sure, it is documented that once an individual is diagnosed with bipolar disorder, that individual has the illness for life. Because one is diagnosed with the disease, it does not mean that one's life has to end. I believe that each passing day the individual with the illness is living and breathing, then that individual is overcoming it by staying alive.

This is why every sufferer of this serious condition should take the "one day at a time" approach. Unfortunately, there are some who have the illness do not envision themselves defeating the disorder. Individuals defeat the disorder by striving to live a long and productive life of consistency.

A consistent life of wellness is what many strive to achieve. In my opinion, a life of wellness is more beneficial to an individual than enormous wealth. If an individual has their health, then that individual is thriving.

Individuals who are experiencing the disease must strive for a life of wellness and wholeness. When consistent wellness and wholeness is maintained, then the bearer overcomes the illness. Maintaining a life of consistency can prove difficult when the depressive person is in the midst of a manic or depressed episode.

I have experienced both manic and depressed episodes. There were times that I did not think that I would ever become well and whole again. After experiencing those episodes, I became determined that I would overcome the disease.

It has been over ten years since I have experienced any type of episode. I am grateful and thankful that I was able to overcome the disorder by making some changes to my thought process. Envisioning a life of consistency and wellness ultimately aided me in overcoming life's stressors.

How one views life internally can make a significant difference. I believe that an individual can either think themselves well or think themselves sick. The mind is extremely powerful. An individual can overcome this severe mental illness by what is said to oneself cognitively.

One way of overcoming any illness is by following doctor's orders. It is imperative that the depressive person take the medication as prescribed. I understand that the majority of the medications prescribed have pronounced side effects.

The most common side effect from taking medication that is prescribed for bipolar disorder is tremors. Tremors can become quite embarrassing, especially, in public. Because of this noticeable side effect, some defy doctor's orders and opt not to take the prescribed medication.

This decision can prove extremely costly. When an individual who has bipolar disorder elects not to take the medicine as prescribed, that individual is ultimately doing more harm to his or herself. Some do not realize that the symptoms of the illness can escalate when the prescribed medicine is not taken.

I must admit that the side effects of the medicine pale in comparison to becoming consistently healthy. Some who have the illness play a game of roulette in regard to their health. When an individual decides not to take their medication, the symptoms of the bearer's illness can become progressively worse.

It took a while for me to accept that I am better off taking the medication. Sure, I do not look forward to the side effects of taking the prescribed medication, but I will sacrifice an embarrassment of a tremor as opposed to having symptoms of the illness.

Taking medication to some can be interpreted as a sign of weakness. In my opinion, I think an individual demonstrates courage by remaining on a prescribed medication regimen. Most doctors are competent in regard to the use and dosage of many medications for bipolar disorder.

Finding a competent psychiatrist who has one's best interest is vital. I believe that the individual who has a positive professional relationship with their psychiatrist will likely take the prescribed medication if trust is established. All who have the illness must incorporate taking their medication into their daily routine.

For example, taking prescribed medication should become just as routine as eating various meals throughout the day. Some depressed persons might have to take their medication one or more times in a given day. Regardless of how often an individual with the disorder must take the prescribed dosage of medication, the bearer of the disorder should not abuse the usage of it.

Many who are diagnosed with a mental illness should not commit the mistake of not taking the medicine when they feel better. This error is commonly committed far too often. Some naively deem themselves well when the symptoms of the illness commences to subside.

Those who are living and coping with the disorder should view the medication as a helper in journeying through life's difficulties. Bearers of the condition must not put their health into jeopardy due to minor side effects. Side effects are a minimal sacrifice if the goal of the depressive person is to remain healthy on a continual basis.

Having bipolar disorder or any other mental illness does not have to become a death sentence. The individual with the disorder has a variety of resources to succeed in life. For example, cognitive therapy with a board certified psychiatrist along with medication management can help the individual excel despite the illness.

Today, the stigma of being bipolar is becoming less of an issue. Sure, there are some who will always doubt that a sufferer will live a successful and prosperous life. In order for an individual to defeat the disorder, that individual must accept the diagnosis.

There are some who spend the majority of their time trying to convince themselves that they do not have the disorder. While the individual is in self-denial, the illness still remains. The first step for any individual in recovery is acceptance.

Although the road to recovery can be difficult to obtain, recovery is not insurmountable. I am certain that many bearers of the illness can and will live a normal life. Living a normal life commences when the individual gains confidence and insight on the symptoms and triggers of the disorder.

I believe that a lifestyle change is also vital in the defeat of the illness. Many who are affected by bipolar disorder might live a reckless lifestyle. One of the symptoms of some with the disorder is high-risk behavior.

It is extremely dangerous to participate in behaviors such as illicit sex and random drug use. These behaviors can also lead to an untimely death. It is imperative that the individual with the disorder make the necessary lifestyle changes to tame or control their dangerous actions.

Sadly, some do not take the proper precautions in order to defeat the illness. After a significant amount of time, the friends and loved ones of the depressive person may lose hope. Before the support of those closest to the sufferer commences to waver, the individual must strive to make a commitment to their mental health.

In my own life, I decided to commit my life to putting my mental health first. I understand that there are people and triggers that contribute to my illness. Because I give my mental health top priority, there are some people and places that I purposely tend to avoid.

When I made the conscious decision to commit to those changes in my life, my condition and illness commenced to improve. In my opinion, a doctor, therapist, or those closest to you can help someone to a certain extent. Recovery from bipolar disorder starts and ends when the individual is accepting and honest with his or herself. The bearer of the disease must be committed to both the treatment of the condition, as well as lifestyle changes.

One must never allow the illness to defeat or stop one from a life of long-term success. Long-term success is not only financial and monetary success, but success is obtained by a life of consistency. Bipolar disorder is not a death sentence when the individual with the disorder has continuous psychological health.

CHAPTER 2

Every Sufferer Is Different

As an individual having bipolar disorder for over twenty-five years, I have learned that some who have the disorder have various levels of severity. There are some who suffer from the illness that is in a worse circumstance than another individual who is diagnosed with the same illness. Many who have the illness will have varying experiences, while others will experience the same type of scenarios.

I have seen some who are diagnosed with the disease that are independent, as well as others who struggle with basic needs. Fortunately, there are various organizations and programs that can assist the individual with acquiring more independence. Some who have the illness fall into a high functioning level of the spectrum.

Individuals on the high-functioning level of the illness have a greater chance of not allowing the disorder to have precedence over their life. These same individuals can hold down a job and journey through life just as well as nonsufferers. I believe that any depressive person, whether high functioning or not, can do anything that they put their mind and heart into.

It all begins with what the individual believes in their heart that they can achieve. In my opinion, achievement and goals is accomplished with the right attitude and mindset. This is not to say that any individual, whether Bipolar or not, cannot obtain any goal without the proper support, but a positive outlook and mindset can do wonders in an individual's life, despite being diagnosed with bipolar disorder.

In regard to my own life, I do not compare my experiences with the illness to others. Although I am aware that some might experience universal symptoms of the disorder, I am also certain that we all experience the world differently. Because of each individual's unique life perspective, it is more beneficial to the individual with the disorder not to become pigeonholed and stereotyped by the nonbearer of the disorder.

If the bearer of bipolar disorder is viewed by the nonbearer on an individualistic basis, then the nonbearer is less likely to group all individuals with the illness in the same category. Some who have the illness might be a co-worker or family member whom you least expect is dealing with the illness. Everyone has various ways of coping with sickness.

We all will experience some sort of illness and sickness. There are a plethora of diseases that currently plague both our world and society, today. bipolar disorder just happens to be one of many illnesses that affect millions worldwide.

Out of the millions that are bearers of the illness, each scenario varies. Not all individuals with this disease are entertaining suicide on a continuous basis. It is imperative that nonsufferers understand that no two sufferers of bipolar disorder will react the same to the same situation and circumstances. This is why God made each and every individual in the world unique.

My initial experience with the illness occurred when I was in college in New Orleans. I can recall how alone I felt, though I had a plethora of friends and associates. Activities that I enjoyed, previously, was no longer appealing to me.

There was a deep sadness that took over my life. The type of sadness that I initially experienced lasted the majority of the semester. I felt like I did not have any support from my family.

In my opinion, family is extremely important. I believe that the support from family can help an individual in life's trials. Because of the lack of support from family, I commenced to have self-pity

When an individual has self-pity, it can lead to unwanted depression. Due to having an enormous amount of self-pity, I needed to find an escape from reality. The type of escape that I chose was indulging in alcohol.

Alcohol, depression, and self-pity ultimately led to my diagnosis of bipolar disorder. At the time that I was indulging in alcohol, I was experiencing the depressed part of the illness. I knew something was wrong when my days of feeling depressed lasted for weeks, then months.

I did not realize that my use of alcohol, eventually, compounded my condition. What I was doing during the time of my alcohol use was self-medicating. In January of 1993, I went to an intimate gathering that would ultimately change my life.

While at that gathering, I can recall how I tried to drink my troubles away. Because I was still a teenager, I did not have the proper coping skills to deal with the lack of family support. So, the way that I dealt with my deep sadness was to overindulge in drinking.

As a result of the poor choice that I made, my mood went from optimistic to hopeless. There were days that I felt that my positive outlook on life would never return. It did not help my mood when I felt abandoned and ostracized by so-called friends and associates that did not have my best interest.

After the semester ended, I returned home. Soon, I commenced to resume the activities that I previously enjoyed. Though I was going out with my friends at that time, mentally I felt that something was different.

One night in August of 1993, I could not sleep. I stayed up all night writing a twenty-page letter to my former girlfriend. My behavior during that time was strange and manic. I can recall how I commenced to walk outside of my house early in the morning for no apparent reason. This was my first experience with a manic mood.

Due to my manic behavior, I knew that I needed help. Soon, I voluntarily checked myself into a mental hospital. This is when the psychiatrist in the hospital diagnosed me with Manic Depression, also known as bipolar disorder. My experience with the disorder might vary from others that also have the illness. The reaction of each individual experiencing the illness will also vary.

Each diagnosis of the disorder must be handled on an individual basis. This means that every individual has varying degrees of the same illness. A psychiatrist that is treating various sufferers should not treat each individual the same.

Now this does not mean that the doctor should play favorites amongst their patients. The goal for treatment varies with each individual's case. There are some who have bipolar disorder that have a plethora of core issues to work through, while some have minimal issues to conquer.

In regard to the amount of medication that each bearer takes, this will also vary. Some may take either more or less medication than others. Also, each medication that is prescribed for each individual will affect each individual in a different way.

A medication that might be prescribed for one individual could have a positive effect, and the same medication taken by another individual could have a negative effect. As a result of each person having a variety of body compositions, I can understand why some medications might affect various bearers in a different manner. When it comes to taking prescribed medicines, a qualified psychiatrist will take the differences amongst other patients into consideration.

There are some psychiatric medications that I have taken in the past that had negative side effects. I can recall how severe my side effects were from taking this one particular medication that I became quite concerned. After conversing with another individual, who had the same condition, about the effects of a particular medication, the individual who also took the same prescribed medicine did not have the same negative reaction.

This is why it is imperative that a depressive person is in tuned with one's body. A bearer must not be timid in revealing to the doctor about negative side effects. There is a trial and error effect in medicine that a doctor must take with each sufferer.

Most psychiatrists will consider the negative effect that some psychiatric medicines pose. Individuals with bipolar disorder must be vocal. The psychiatrist should empathize with their patients.

Those who have the disease must not be silent. Although some are timid in revealing to their doctor how the medication is affecting them, others are not. Some will instantly inform their doctor on how the medicine is affecting them.

If you are a bearer of bipolar disorder, strive not to become alarmed with how much medication that another individual is taking. One's focus must be on one's own treatment and medicine management. One must become cognizant that each individual has vast severity levels of one's illness.

One depressive person may need more medication, compared with another bearer, in order to cope and deal with the stresses in life. Only the certified psychiatrist knows the reason why one patient is prescribed more medicine than another person. The reality is that each individual will typically not take the same medicines, as well as the same amount of dosage.

It is human nature to become inquisitive about how others with the same condition are coping with it. Sometimes an individual with the same illness can gain inspiration. Individuals who are coping with bipolar disorder should learn about the disorder not only from a doctor, but also from others who share the same condition as well.

There are support groups for those who are experiencing mental illness. NAMI (National Alliance for the Mentally Ill) is one example of a variety of organizations that can assist individuals with bipolar disorder. With the increase in individuals with mental illness, there is also a greater chance that an individual will have an opportunity to relate to others who are also experiencing mental illness.

At the time of my diagnosis, I was fortunate to have access to support groups that specialized in my particular condition. I felt that I was not alone. Although some of the members of the support groups had different experiences with the disorder, it was imperative to my overall improvement that I learned from other individuals who have been dealing with the illness for a substantial amount of time.

Previously, I discussed how the majority of individuals experiencing the disorder could experience varying degrees of severity. Some have greater control over one's condition than others. I believe that an individual who is struggling with the illness could acquire tools from other individuals who have learned how to cope with the condition.

When I attended various support groups with other bearers of bipolar disorder, I noticed the diverseness of each individual sufferer. There were some who were affluent, while others were middle class to less fortunate. Other individuals were from other ethnicities.

I learned from interacting with other individuals who have the illness that it does not affect any one specific gender or ethnic group in particular. From my experience with others with the disorder, I learned what other bearers did to combat the disorder. This is when I realized that every individual have their own unique way of coping with stress.

My way of coping with stressors in life might not be beneficial to the way that another individual might cope with the same stressful situation. Some chose to participate in activities that can compound stress, while other individuals learn over time, what to do and what not to do. How a depressive person deals mentally with stress can contribute to an individual not succumbing to the illness reigning in one's life.

Every individual with the disorder can learn from others who have mastered the triggers of the condition. This illness can become difficult to overcome. Those who desire to learn from other bearers must also incorporate their own way of overcoming the illness. In regard to bipolar disorder, there is something that an individual can learn from another individual with the illness in spite of differences.

When I was initially diagnosed with this illness, my life was in dire straits. At the time of my diagnosis, I did not foresee that my mental health would improve. Honestly, I thought that my life was over.

The friends and associates who were in my life during that time were prospering. Some of my peers were getting married and finishing college. While they were achieving their goals, I was struggling to stay well.

It seemed as though everything that could go wrong in my life came into fruition. Because of my illness, I could not complete the goals that I set. One of the goals that I desired to achieve was to complete college.

Before the onset of my illness, I had a clear path to achieving various goals. I was on pace to completing college on time. When an individual is going through the various moods of bipolar disorder, everything else in life takes a backseat.

This is not to say that an individual who is a bearer of the illness cannot obtain the same goals and achievements as nonsufferers. In fact, an individual who has the disease can prosper. The individual only has his or herself to convince in order to attain their goals.

Once the depressive person realizes that it does not matter how many setbacks that one has in life, one must never give up. I understand that it might be easier for some to realize their goals and dreams than others. An individual with the disorder must never use their illness as an excuse to never strive to achieve.

Some with the disease make the mistake of listening to their own doubts and insecurities. Individuals who listen to thoughts of self-doubt will not prosper in life until they cease from comparisons. There is a plethora of sufferers that view others as successful while not believing in oneself.

What constitutes a successful life? I believe that a successful individual should not be in competition with others. Success for an individual with bipolar disorder is when the individual realizes one's own self-worth. Those who are worthy do not feel jealous or inferior when others prosper or succeed.

Though I have suffered from this illness for many years, I believe that my own life commenced to prosper when I ceased from comparing my life with others. I realized that I could only become the best person that I could be and no one else. The only thing that I can do in life is to give my all in all that I do.

We all are journeying through life at varying paces. Some move at a more rapid pace, while others navigate through life at a slower pace. In this life, there are no any right or wrong answers in regard to how an individual chooses to live their life, as long as the individual lives their life abiding the law. In this society, an individual owes it to oneself to preserve one's own health and success. A bearer of bipolar disorder should not become discouraged by the prosperity of others in any capacity.

Have you ever received unfavorable news? When an individual is initially diagnosed with bipolar disorder, the individual can react in two ways. One way that an individual might react to the diagnosis of illness is with great sadness and shame. Another way that an individual might react to the diagnosis is with extreme determination and optimism.

Now I am not saying that one should jump for joy when diagnosed with the illness because it is unrealistic. Bipolar disorder is a serious mental illness that can ruin an individual's life. Many who suffer from the illness do not envision a life of joy and victory over the disorder.

In fact, the majority of individuals with the illness allow the illness to defeat them in some capacity. Some never recover from what a doctor or society has told them about the disease. It is a sickness that will defeat the individual who remains in the state of hopelessness.

After my initial diagnosis, I did not know what to do. It was revealed to me by several doctors that there is no cure for the disorder. How does an individual react to a doctor telling them that there is not any hope to having a cure? An individual can continue in a life of hopelessness or attack the illness with confidence and determination.

Yes, it is true that each individual with the disorder has different experiences, but I believe that the individual with disorder can mentally make a decision. I believe that the affected individual can take all the medicine in the world, but the medicine will not have any effect if the individual is not optimistic mentally. A positive mental outlook in spite of unfavorable odds can work wonders in a depressive person's life.

I can recall how I was not always optimistic about tackling the disease. There was a time that I allowed others to limit me due to the illness. Some thought that I could not achieve various goals because of my diagnosis.

Ultimately, I graduated college and became a writer in spite of what others thought that I could not do. Defying the odds of not allowing bipolar disorder to overwhelm one's life is not easy to obtain. It may take the bearer several years to gain the right type of mindset to combat the illness.

Although the individual with the illness may have common symptoms with other individuals, one's optimism and mental outlook is what separates some who are thriving in spite of the illness, compared to others who are not thriving. Personally, I have experienced many obstacles as a result of having bipolar disorder. Once I changed my mental outlook on life, the illness became less of a factor.

All bearers of bipolar disorder share the same prognosis that there is not any cure for the disease. One could allow the fact that a doctor gave them a grim diagnosis to defeat them or rise to the occasion. The difference between those with the illness that are setting and accomplishing goals and others who are not is simply one's attitude and mindset.

Behavior is vital in regard to this illness. Some demonstrate anger, while others want to buy everything in sight. Typically, an individual who over spends for no reason at all might be considered as manic.

This behavior can lead to financial ruin. Many consider an individual who overspends for no apparent reason as exhibiting self-destructive behavior. I am aware that not all who are affected by bipolar disorder will over spend.

Anger is another behavior that I have seen in other individuals with the disorder. Personally, I came in contact with another bearer who displayed uncontrollable anger. I can recall how irritable and sensitive that this particular individual was.

He was screaming at the top of his lungs. Also, he found any reason to express his angry feelings toward others. I must admit that I was a little taken back about the enormous anger of this particular individual.

In my experience with having the sickness, I did not demonstrate the type of anger as the individual who I just discussed. In fact, I experienced the polar opposite of anger, which is sadness. There are not any individuals with this illness that will demonstrate the same type of mood at the same time.

Of course, I am not a doctor or psychiatrist, but I have been in the company of other sufferers. It is through my interaction with other individuals who I realized that each individual with this particular illness is different. Before I was in the company of the individual who was extremely irritable and upset, I was unaware that irritability was one of the symptoms of the disorder.

One of the symptoms of bipolar disorder that I previously experienced was overspending. I was unaware of my behavior, but it was brought to my attention. I can recall buying things that I did not need.

Today, I must say that I do not overspend anymore. Now I am more practical in regard to my spending. Also, I use to engage in impulsive and high-risk behavior. When I acted in that self-destructive behavior, I did not realize the impact that it would potentially have on my life.

The individual who demonstrated great anger and irritability may not have a problem with overspending as I had. On the contrary, I never had an anger and irritability issue. Some with this illness are less destructive than others.

This particular illness affects each individual in various ways. Although an individual may not have an anger and irritability issue, it does not mean that the individual does not suffer from the illness. The goal for every bearer of this disorder is to become whole and healthy.

All who have this illness must become cognizant of their own behavior. Those who are closest to the individual can account and pinpoint the bearer's actions. Hopefully, the individual with the condition can become knowledgeable about how this illness affects themselves, as well as other bearers in various ways.

Thus far, I have stated that each individual has various experiences with the illness. Bipolar disorder is an illness that can become devastating in an individual's life. It is imperative that the bearer has someone in their life that will journey through the highs and lows of the disorder.

From my perspective, I did not receive a ton of support from a plethora of family members. On my mother's side of the family, I have a numerous amount of cousins. There are not many of them who have reached out to me when they received the news that I have a mental illness.

As a member of an African-American family, the majority of the members do not desire to see a doctor. So instead of seeking professional help, some would rather live with a sickness instead of going to a doctor. I believe that mental illness affects a plethora of members of the African-American community.

Many of its members refuse to acknowledge that they have a mental health issue. Due to lack of acknowledgment of a potential mental problem, the condition can worsen if left untreated. With any health condition, it is imperative that the individual does not put their potential condition on the backburner.

Because mental illness is viewed as a sign of weakness in the African-American community, many of its members will suffer internally. Some members of this community are more concerned with keeping up a façade, then taking the time to seek help. This is the difference between members of the African-American community in comparison with other ethnicities.

I believe that my condition would not have improved if I chose to not seek professional help for the illness. Internally, I knew that something was not right within me. It would have been unwise for me to have the same view as other members of my ethnic community in regard to seeing a physician.

Minority sufferers of bipolar disorder might have more of an uphill battle than other members of other racial groups. It is a known fact that minorities are less likely to consult a physician due to lack of trust. Also, many minorities would rather endure the symptoms of a potential illness because they might be fearful of the outcome.

When it comes to an individual's health, as well as one's mental health, it is something that must not become overlooked. It is imperative that an individual who feels that they might be suffering mentally, listen to their intuition. If one's intuition is telling one that they may need help, do not disregard it.

Individuals in various minority communities should not ostracize those who have mental health conditions. There will always be illnesses and conditions that will plague individuals regardless of what ethic background that one is a part of. All people are not the same, and this is why members of minority communities who are nondepressive persons of bipolar disorder or any other mental illness should embrace those who are affected by it and treat them with empathy.

Through my experience with having bipolar disorder, I have encountered good doctors and not so good ones. There was some who had my best interest, while others seemed uncaring. Some would equate it to having a good bedside manner.

I am aware that individuals who are experiencing this psychiatric condition or any other type of mental illness can become challenging at times. It takes a special doctor to deal with the various moods of bearers. Sometimes individuals who are diagnosed with bipolar disorder can become violent.

Psychiatrists who deal with patients who are physically violent must be commended. There are some individuals with the illness who can also become verbally abusive. Doctors who care for those who are abusive both physically and verbally are expected to demonstrate great restraint.

Personally, I have not seen a psychiatrist fall victim to physical violence from a patient, but I am certain that it occurs. I can recall how a particular psychiatrist would appear like he was involved in an altercation. After this particular doctor had seen this one patient, I remembered how his hair and clothes were out of sorts.

Judging from the way this doctor appeared physically, I could tell that a patient became violent with him. The doctor who was a victim of violence was an extremely kind man. Physically, the doctor was diminutive in stature.

From my experience with this doctor, I could tell that he was caring. I believe that physical violence is unacceptable. No one should ever become violent toward another individual.

Individuals with this illness who become violent toward a psychiatrist do not have any regard to the value of a caring doctor. While there are some who have little regard for the value of therapy, there are some who embrace it. Psychiatrists are not just doctors who prescribe psychiatric medication. A good and reliable psychiatrist is also concerned with their patient's welfare.

They will go above and beyond the call of duty. I understand that there are some psychiatrists who do not care to learn the daily activities of their patients. Unfortunately, there are some psychiatrists who do not have their patient's interest at heart.

When I was initially diagnosed with this disease, I did not value the care of a reliable psychiatrist. I only viewed these doctors as legal pill pushers. As I have gained more experience interacting with psychiatrists, I have learned to value the psychiatrist who is concerned with my overall health.

I believe that an individual who is receiving help from a competent doctor must value it. Some who are coping with bipolar disorder are never satisfied with their doctor's care regardless of the amount of support that the doctor demonstrates. The difference between an individual who improves from this disorder, as opposed to another individual who does not improve is the value that the individual places on therapy from a competent and reliable doctor.

In my opinion, there is not any excuse for an individual with bipolar disorder or any other mental illness to not seek help. Thankfully, help is available for those who really desire it. Unlike previous years, the stigma of having a mental disorder is becoming less of an issue for the sufferer.

Although there are available resources for the individual with the illness, some will choose not to take advantage of it. I am aware that each individual with the disorder may experience it from various perspectives. Each bearer of the disorder has a unique experience with the illness.

Bipolar disorder affects each individual in various ways. The illness can affect some positively or negatively. Some who are diagnosed choose to allow the disorder to have precedence over their lives, while others are defeating the illness by living a prosperous life.

After receiving news from my former psychiatrist that I have bipolar disorder, I decided to live as normal a life as possible. Also, I never allowed the illness to be used as an excuse to not accomplish dreams and goals. Because of this mindset, I, along with help from the Creator, have been able to see many of the goals and dreams that I set come to pass.

I believe that because I did not allow this sickness to dominate my life, I have been able to realize goals that were in the embryonic stage. One's attitude and mindset is usually the difference between individuals who are successful as oppose to those who are not. Those with the illness must not allow themselves to prove those who are nonbearers right when nonbearers think that the individual cannot accomplish anything.

A bearer proves a nonbearer of the disorder right by not taking initiative in accomplishing goals that are set. I have seen it time after time others with the disorder using their illness as an excuse not to dream big. Just because an individual may have an obstacle in having a severe mental illness, known as bipolar disorder, does not mean that the individual should cease from living.

I will be the first to admit that I am not superior to any other individual, but I believe the difference between myself and another individual who might have the same disease is my refusal to have a defeatist attitude. There are some individuals who are experiencing the disorder that are allowing life to pass them by. Day after day, individuals with this mindset are only going through the motions.

Sadly, many with this illness will allow what society and the opinion of others to defeat them. Those with this disorder should strive to become different than others that allowed the illness to take their happiness and joy. It takes a plethora of courage to become different. Because bearers of bipolar disorder are viewed differently by society, each individual with the illness must not allow what society deems as normal to cause them to succumb to the moods, stressors, and the pressure of the disorder.

CHAPTER 3

View Yourself Positively

Self-confidence can become a struggle for many. It can become difficult to obtain when an individual basis one's confidence in worldly things. Inner and self-confidence can become fragile when someone has an illness such as bipolar disorder.

There are some who are continuously reminded by others of their condition. When an individual is constantly aware of their condition, it can way heavy on one's self-esteem. The individual who views one's self-worth by others' negative opinion and stereotype of having mental illness will struggle with confidence.

In my opinion, self-confidence is something that is acquired. It is also extremely unwavering and unpredictable like the wind. An individual might be confident one day, and on the next day, the same individual might lose it.

If having confidence is difficult for an individual who does not suffer from mental illness. Think about the confidence of an individual who has mental illness. Society has a way of labeling its members. The opinions of society will weigh heavily on the psyche of an individual who is only identified as having a psychological condition.

In regard to an individual having any type of psychiatric disorder, usually there are negative references. Some will label the individual as *crazy* or *insane* rather than creative or intelligent. Once someone is identified and labeled negatively, one's confidence is typically destroyed.

What does a negative label do to any individual? A negative label by others will result in a negative and poor self-image. Having a poor self-image of oneself can become dangerous. This negative mindset of oneself could worsen the condition of an individual with mental illness.

It is imperative that bearers of bipolar disorder have the right type of support system. It is an illness that can have one question one's confidence and worth. The individual with the disorder should always seek to be in the company of those who positively edify them.

One cannot view oneself in a positive manner when those who are closest to the depressive person are in a negative state of mind. Individuals who have a negative aura surrounding them are never beneficial to anyone, whether one has a mental condition or not. The environment surrounding the individual with the disease must be filled with empathy and love.

Any individual who is surrounded with love and compassion from those closest to them have a chance to thrive in society. We live in a world that is usually unkind to individuals who have mental challenges. It can become difficult to have self-confidence when society as a whole says that the individual with a psychiatric disorder should feel inferior. In the end, the only thing that should matter to the individual with the illness is one's own image of oneself.

There was a time in my life that I did not view myself positively. My self-esteem was at an all-time low. I was in danger of allowing the disorder to defeat me. Because I was diagnosed with a mental illness, I thought that my life was over.

One day, my mother came home with this tape series entitled, "The Power of Positive Thinking." At the time that I received these tapes, I was in desperate need of a confidence boost. After listening to the series of tapes by the late great Dr. Norman Vincent Peale, I commenced to develop a positive view of myself.

I will be the first one to tell you that truly viewing oneself positively does not happen overnight. Some who have an excessive overflow of bravado could be viewed as being arrogant and overconfident. Those who demonstrate overconfidence typically have an over inflated view of oneself.

I believe that there is not anything wrong with loving all of oneself. The problem with an individual with too much self-love is that the individual with this mindset is incapable of unconditionally loving others. In regard to individuals who have the illness, some bearers struggle with basic confidence.

I am aware that some with the disorder have what is called "delusions of grandeur." Individuals who display this mindset are described as having grandiose thoughts and behavior. Individuals who demonstrate this behavior will typically think of themselves as a movie star, millionaire, or someone who is deemed important in society.

Although some who have bipolar disorder are grandiose, it does not mean that the individual is confident. In fact, I believe that an individual who has to pretend to be self-important is struggling internally with confidence. The majority of individuals with *bravado* are not confident at all.

Most who behave in this fashion are hiding behind a façade. Furthermore, I believe that some who behave in this fashion are over-compensating for lack of faith in oneself. On the other end of the spectrum, there are some with the disease who do not exhibit grandiose behavior.

There are some who are bearers of bipolar disorder that do not display overinflated confidence. In fact, some succumb to lack of it. For some with the disorder, it can become a task just to face another day. Some who have the illness do not wake up each day with confidence because they view themselves as bipolar.

When a depressive person views oneself as bipolar, it can wane on one's overall self-image. This does not mean that the individual who has bipolar disorder should allow the illness to define them as a person. An individual's overall self-worth is more than an illness. Do not allow oneself to succumb to what society views as normal to impact one's overall self-esteem.

There were times that I had extremely low points due to this illness. Before my condition from the disorder improved, my condition seemed like it worsened. I must admit that there was a point in which my prognosis as a result of the illness looked extremely bleak.

I never thought that I could regain confidence within myself. The road to having a positive self-image started when I dedicated my life to God. I believe that my relationship with Him and His Son, Jesus Christ, made the world of difference in my life.

Although the world and society was telling me that I am bipolar, I gradually commenced to view myself as a child of God. I firmly believe that anything is possible when one believes in God. Judging from my previous episodes and behavior due to having this severe mental disorder, I would probably be the most unlikely individual to overcome this illness.

As I previously stated, bipolar disorder is a serious mental condition that can defeat anyone. Unfortunately, some succumb to the disorder by committing suicide. If the individual who is affected by this illness does not have a relationship with the Creator, then there is a great chance that the illness will overtake the individual.

I understand that everyone is not spiritual. We all have a choice in life about serving God Almighty. In my opinion, seeing a psychiatrist and medication management is vital to the well-being of the individual with the disease. I believe that a right relationship with the heavenly Father and His Son, Jesus Christ, can also help an individual to face anything that one might encounter in this world.

When an individual has a sincere relationship with the Creator, then there is not anything that they cannot achieve. Trusting and having faith in God Almighty will help improve an individual's confidence and self-image. Acquiring a positive view of oneself does not happen hastily.

Once someone identifies oneself as a follower of God, then one's confidence will come from Him. An individual can read a plethora of self-help books to increase one's self image, but only a relationship with God will have a lasting effect. Confidence in God is the key to obtaining inner confidence.

In my experience of having a negative self-image, I was on the brink of utter hopelessness. I can recall how I was going through the motions in life. Life was not enjoyable for me during that time.

My inner confidence and self-image commenced to improve when I sought God wholeheartedly. I submitted myself to God after losing hope that I could improve from having a mental illness. When doctors thought that my overall condition would cause me to initially succumb to it, I gradually lost confidence. After developing a consistent prayer life for many years, I owe my overall improvement and positive self-image to a personal and right relationship with God.

At the time that I was initially diagnosed, I did not have a clue about how to cope with the daily pressures of the world. I did not have an adequate amount of life experience. In other words, I was still learning how to navigate through life.

It took an enormous amount of years for me to develop a positive image of myself. Most individuals who are teenagers lack the growth and maturity to cope with a significant illness. In my teenage state of mind, I did not have any clue about maintaining a positive perception of myself while having a significant mental disorder.

The way that I eventually developed a positive image of myself was by taking the time to getting to know who I am as an individual. There were some people and things in my life that I had to refrain from in order to feel positive internally. I believe that we all should take the time to assess oneself.

While assessing oneself, one can develop a deep love for oneself. This type of deep love for oneself can be obtained through having various trials. An individual with bipolar disorder will not be void of difficulties.

If the bearer of the disorder can endure the pitfalls of the illness, I am certain that the individual can develop self-love. In order for an individual to view oneself positively, it commences and ends with what one tells oneself mentally. I believe that if an individual thinks in their thoughts that they are a negative and unworthy person, then this mindset will influence one into having self-hatred.

Although God Almighty has the ultimate control in everyone's life, each individual has the ultimate control on what they think of oneself mentally. It is very true that if one does not love oneself, it is difficult to love someone else. No one but the individual within has continuous access to you twenty-four hours within a day.

Sufferers of bipolar disorder or any other mental illness have greater odds of developing self-hatred than nonsufferers. Society already tells the individual with the illness that they do not belong. Teenagers and many adults who are diagnosed with this illness sometimes feel ostracized and outcast.

Our world and society can be extremely rude and coldhearted. Sadly, there are many members of society who lack empathy. Some think that as long as the illness is not affecting them personally, then who cares.

Because of the nonempathetic attitude of others, it is imperative that the bearer of bipolar disorder takes the time to get to know all of the positive attributes of oneself. This world can become cruel and heartless. It is a bad combination when society as a whole has little regard for you, and you have little regard for yourself.

Some who are affected by mental illness think that they do not matter. Those who do not take the time to learn oneself will develop a negative self-image. A positive self-image should not be left up to what society as a whole thinks about you.

Negativity should have no place amongst anyone. In the state of our world and society, it is everywhere. From the time that an individual awakens in the morning until the time that an individual retires to bed, negativity is commonplace.

It can become difficult to maintain a positive attitude and mindset when surrounded by negativity. Individuals who are affected by bipolar disorder must strive to gain a positive mindset despite what is happening in the world. When a bearer is affected by the world around them, it can become detrimental to one's overall mindset.

I believe that the increase of individuals affected by bipolar disorder has gained prominence due to the negative impact of society. Because of our society's moral decline, it is easy to succumb to a negative mindset. People are not as friendly and loving as in years past.

It seems as though negativity is becoming progressively worse in our world and society with each passing day. I understand how one's environment can play a role in an individual's negative self-image. Crime is becoming common even amongst neighborhoods that were previously thought of as safe.

Due to the increase of crime and corruption in society as a whole, there are many who are losing faith and hope. As a result of hopelessness, some are turning to all sorts of mind-altering substances. In my opinion, when an individual abuses mind-altering substances, it can have a negative effect on an individual's overall self-esteem.

No one can view them self positively when they are under the influence of some type of substance. The substances can gain control over an individual's mind, thus, affecting an individual's self-image. Once the mind becomes affected and influenced by mind-altering substances, the individual will have little regard for oneself.

Individuals who truly have genuine self-esteem and confidence will not escape from the negativity of the world and society by using any type of substance. I can recall how I would attempt to escape my problems by drinking alcohol. In hindsight, this was a poor decision that eventually affected my overall mental health.

I did not know that my temporary decision to drink alcohol while I was a teenager would take years for me to develop overall confidence. Before I commenced to drink alcohol, I did not have any symptoms of having a mental illness. I believe that my use of alcohol contributed to me having mental illness, as well as lack of confidence. After over twenty years of not consuming an alcoholic beverage, I have regained the confidence within in spite of the negativity that occurs daily in the world.

My suggestion to the individuals who are trying to escape the negativity of one's environment and society is to not use any mind-altering substances to escape. It does not help solve one's problems because when the effects from these substances wear off, one's problems are still current. Pronounced use of these substances will ultimately negatively affect one's mental health and overall positive image. Do not allow the negativity of the world and society to creep into your life because it can become like a cancer to your overall positive outlook of oneself.

Feeling confident in oneself can become a gradual process. There are no shortcuts in an individual acquiring healthy self-esteem. Confidence in oneself should not come at the expense of others.

I can recall how some of the acquaintances in my past would verbally tear one another down. When this occurred, I would become bothered by the negativity. The individuals who participated in insulting one another would find something about the intended target that would make the person feel self-conscious or insecure.

Insults from others can have a negative effect on one's self-confidence. One has to be strong mentally to face unwanted insults and criticism. Sometimes one can become influenced internally about what others say and think about them.

The need for acceptance and approval is prevalent in many. It is in our human nature to want approval from others. If one does not receive approval from others particularly at an early age, it can have a negative effect on one's psyche.

This world can become cruel to some who have not gained acceptance of oneself. As a result of an individual not having a positive image of oneself, questionable and self-destructive behavior commences to take effect. This behavior can lead to an individual having bipolar disorder or any other type of mental illness.

Since I have matured in life, I have come to the realization that what someone chooses to enter one's mind can become powerful. What an individual formulates in one's mind can be the difference between one's own self-approval and nonapproval. In regard to an individual experiencing mental illness, there will always have individuals who do not approve of those that suffer from it.

The stigma of having a mental illness such as bipolar disorder is gradually evaporating, but there is still a negative perception amongst some in society. Individuals who are affected by the illness cannot wait for others' approval. The approval must come from the individual internally.

The depressive person must have a keen focus on gaining approval and confidence from themselves. The world and society as a whole unfortunately will not always grant approval. Those who are bearers of the disorder should not allow the stigma, as well as insults from others, to derail their confidence.

Others can tell someone to be confident, but confidence does not come into fruition until someone formulates a positive self-image within one's mind. It is true that an individual is who he thinks he or she is. This is why it is imperative that an individual affected by the illness do all they can to acquire a lasting positive self-image.

In my opinion, an individual does not have to allow the approval from others in society to dictate one's confidence. If a sufferer of the disorder is waiting for the acceptance of others, they could be waiting for a very long time. At the end of the day, what should matter to the individual affected by the condition is one's own ultimate self-approval.

When I was in my early adulthood years, I must admit that the approval of others became vital to my overall image of myself. It mattered to me about what others thought of me. I naively thought that the approval of my so-called friends at the time would give me validation.

Now I am not saying that the opinion of one's parents or closest relatives does not matter because the opinion of one's family should matter. Although the opinion of one's family is important, they cannot live one's life. At the end of the day, what matters is how you view yourself.

I believe that a supportive family can be beneficial in an individual having a positive perception of oneself. Positive reinforcement from the family of an individual suffering from bipolar disorder is imperative. When the family of the individual who is affected is instilling confidence, then the individual does not have any choice but to become confident.

As for myself, I have stated how I struggled with inner confidence early in life. Though it might have seemed that I was confident amongst my group of friends at that time, in reality, I was not. The confidence that I exhibited during that specific time in my life was not genuine.

On the surface, I might have seemed confident, but internally I was in total disarray. The thoughts that I thought toward myself were not positive. Because I was superficial in my own confidence, this led to me viewing myself negatively.

Essentially, I was faking it until I made it. Society suggests that an individual pretends to be confident although they are far from it. I do not agree that an individual should have a façade of confidence.

In my opinion, an individual is doing more harm to his or herself when they pretend to be something that they are not. I believe that an individual who is struggling with inner confidence learns how to become honest from within. If one is having a difficult time with becoming confident, I suggest that one learn how to pinpoint one's own positive qualities and attributes.

This process will take a significant amount of time. The goal for every individual who is affected by this illness is to gain and remain confident in life. Confidence commences when an individual maintains a positive self-image regardless of the troubles and difficulties that are surrounding them.

Those who are affected by bipolar disorder must not listen to the negative stigma of having a mental illness. In order to acquire and maintain confidence for the individual who is suffering from the disorder, the bearer must take a daily approach to the process. This will require an enormous amount of patience.

I am certain that many have heard the saying that Rome was not built in one day. The same can be said in regard to the acquisition of confidence. Genuine and real inner confidence requires patience and courage.

Because of my illness, I went through a plethora of trials. I was hospitalized several times between 1997 to 2000. Due to my multiple hospitalizations, it became difficult to sustain any continuity in my life.

As a result, I could not accomplish many of the goals that I had set during that time. I can recall dropping out of college multiple times due to my illness. It seemed as though the illness was getting the best of me.

My life was spiraling before my eyes, and I had to do something. One day, I met up with a friend. We agreed to meet up at a little Christian store on the edge of downtown Houston. The reason why we met at the store is because I wanted to obtain a Bible.

I am grateful and thankful that my friend bought me my first Bible because by reading it my life began to transform. When I initially read the Word of God, I did not realize how much it would help me with my illness. Initially, I did not understand how daily reading of the Word of God could help with every trial that one encounters.

I believe that my mindset and attitude toward myself gradually changed because I commenced to read the Bible daily. The Word of God is a book that all can draw inspiration from. It is a book that was inspired by men and women of God through the influence of God Almighty, Himself.

If an individual who is affected by bipolar disorder commits to daily reading of the Word of God, I am certain that the disorder will not defeat them. Although one may read the Bible daily, it does not mean that the individual will be instantly cured from having a mental disorder. I am only suggesting that an individual who is a regular reader of God's Word has a chance of viewing oneself positively.

As a believer in God, I have faith that God can do the impossible. If I did not commit to reading the Word of God, I probably would not wholeheartedly believe that God Himself, through His Word, could transform an individual with little inner confidence to an individual with confidence from God. Confidence from God is not the same as worldly confidence.

Worldly confidence only works on a superficial level. In other words, confidence that is acquired and obtained from someone other than God is not long lasting. When an individual who suffers from any type of illness comes to the realization that God is truly on their side, then they will be able to have godly confidence.

Godly confidence is extremely powerful. It takes time to acquire the confidence that only God Almighty can give. Sometimes an individual will have to encounter various difficulties and trials in order to develop genuine confidence.

Depressive individuals must strive to have a genuine relationship with the Most High. Prayer does help with having a relationship with the Creator, but by reading His Word on a continuous basis, an individual can learn how to develop inner confidence that will be sustainable despite having a psychiatric condition.

Some unfortunately journey through this, at times, difficult life without truly loving oneself. All who have a mental illness should strive for self-love. I am not talking about the self-love that borders on arrogance.

When an individual with bipolar disorder can accept his or herself despite having the illness, then a huge breakthrough will result from the individual having self-love. Individuals with this illness must not allow the disorder to defeat them by hating oneself. It is imperative that the bearer avoids the negative stigma of what society says.

In my own battle with the disease, I never allowed the stigma of the illness to dictate how I should view myself. Sure, there were times in my life that I struggled with having inner confidence. As I stated previously, I attribute my confidence to God Almighty and the daily reading of His Word.

I believe that my decision to follow God and His Son wholeheartedly transformed the way I ultimately viewed myself. Basically, I made the decision to have faith in what the Word of God says about me as opposed to what a doctor or society thinks. After I made up my mind personally to not allow what others' opinion of me affect the way I viewed myself, eventually I viewed myself positively.

We live in a world and society that is image conscious. Sadly, society bases an individual's self-worth on one's outer appearance rather than one's heart. The individual with the disorder must carefully get their mind and heart in check.

I understand that it might be easy for others to say that a depressive person must work on themselves. As an individual with a major mental illness, I can understand how resentment toward nonsufferers can formulate. Some who are unaffected by a psychological disorder have no clue about what it is like when one's mind and thoughts betray them. Those who are not affected do not understand how the stigma of having a mental illness can deeply hurt the individual who is affected, thus, resulting in the bearer's overall negative self-image.

Many point out the negative shortcomings in others, rather than lifting others up. In this overall negative society in which we live, some chose to accept the negative view of society's perception. Bearers will not have a positive image of oneself, along with inner confidence when the individual does not become immune to society's opinion.

Individuals with bipolar disorder must learn to accept and recognize their shortcomings while having inner confidence and self-love. Those affected by the illness cannot develop these qualities without the support from friends, family, spiritual belief, and faith. Earlier I discussed how each individual with the disorder is different.

A positive self-image and true inner confidence will always vary amongst others. Individuals who have the illness should not live as doormats. All who are experiencing this disorder are just as important to God than those who are not affected by it. Once an individual who has the disease realizes that their worth in life is vital, then they become empowered, thus, resulting in confidence.

Bearers that are affected by bipolar disorder can view themselves positively. In order to develop a positive self-image of oneself, it will take the support of positive friends and family. Also, a genuine spiritual relationship with the heavenly Father will also help one develop healthy self-esteem.

I am aware that some with the disorder will not always have the support from family and friends. In my case, I can recall how my mother did not give up on me while I was battling the disorder. Because she was supportive of me despite my illness, it gave me the incentive to strive to overcome the illness.

There were times in my experience with the disease that I felt defeated by it. I thought to myself during that negative time in my life that I was the illness itself. This mindset affected my overall view of myself.

When doctors and others revealed that I suffered from bipolar disorder, it had a negative effect on my confidence. Due to the opinion of others, I became bipolar. Although it was the illness that I would bear, it never told the whole story about who I was as an individual.

I made up in my mind that though I have this particular illness, I would make it my life's mission not to allow others to dictate how I should feel about the person from within. Although society and others may have an opinion about how an individual with bipolar disorder would act and behave, I decided that I would love and respect myself in spite of the negative image that comes from some nonbearers who do not have any regard for affected individuals.

After I realized that my life was valuable, I commenced to view myself positively. Once an individual begins to value life, that same individual will commence to value oneself. When an individual values something in life, that person will go above and beyond to preserve it and protect it.

Individuals affected by the illness will view oneself positively when they become in tuned with who they are in their core. Becoming familiar with oneself requires great self-reflection, as well as intense self-examination. Some chose not to become acquainted with oneself out of fear that intense examination will reveal negative flaws and shortcomings.

Everyone has attractive qualities. Some are unaware about the quality person that lives just beneath the surface. For many, it is easier to recognize the negative qualities that are living within in us as opposed to positive qualities.

Real and true confidence does not occur when an individual is not honest with oneself. Those who have the illness should not allow the negative aspects of the illness to define the core person within. Once the sufferer values one's core self, then they will view oneself positively.

CHAPTER 4

Developing Peace of Mind

Peace of mind is something that many find difficult to obtain. We live in a world and society that is constantly in chaos and deep turmoil. Every day there is always a surprising threat of violence in an unsuspecting neighborhood.

Many who are experiencing the illness are usually striving to maintain and develop one's peace of mind. The individual might have to contend with racing thoughts, which is one of the symptoms of the disorder. As a bearer, I can recall a time in which I had racing thoughts.

My mind was in constant overdrive. At the time that I was experiencing racing thoughts, I did not foresee a time in my life that my mind would be at peace. The racing thoughts that I experienced came as a result from worry and busyness.

I was trying to do too much. Because I was constantly on the go, I had little time to rest. My life at that time was between school and trying to attend every party and nightclub that I could.

During that time in my life, peace of mind did not seem attainable. I had to be in the action of the nightlife. I blindly and naively thought that I would become fulfilled by this fast-paced lifestyle.

I believe that the majority of individuals who are participating in a fast-paced lifestyle are searching for peace of mind in all the wrong places. Many who participate in that way of living will not obtain inner peace. In my opinion, peace of mind does not come as a result of a life of continuous partying.

Real peace of mind is developed when one's mind is clear. The individual with the disorder must strive to acquire peace in one's mind. This can become a lifelong process for some.

There are some nonsufferers of the illness that never acquire peace in their mind. One cannot develop and obtain peace by putting mind-altering substances in one's body. Some who partake in the use of these substances naively think that these substances will allow them to escape from reality and find peace.

It is true that recreational activities that an individual views as fun can help the individual with peace. Everyone, including individuals affected by the illness, must learn how to find the balance between reality and pleasure. It is never good to have too much of anything because it can result in dysfunction.

In my own life, I have learned to develop balance in life. The way that I acquired peace of mind was by incorporating exercise and wholesome recreation to my life of activities. After years of consistency in this process, I attribute my lifestyle changes for helping me to develop peace of mind despite being affected by a psychological illness.

The Word of God has been instrumental in my improvement from this disease. I attribute my recovery from the symptoms of the illness to God's Word. Before my recovery, there was little hope from some of the doctors and others that my overall condition would improve.

In my mind, I knew that I had to rely on something other than a doctor and group therapy to get me through having the disorder. I made the conscious decision to read the Word of God to help me overcome the difficulties of the illness. My peace of mind from reading God's Word daily was not immediate.

There were times in which I encountered various trials because of the illness. Some think that their problems and trials will disappear because they are striving to become closer to God. In some cases, trials and problems will increase when an individual decides to live for the Creator.

I believe that a bearer of the disorder must develop faith that they will acquire the peace of mind that is needed to overcome it. It seems as though turmoil is the embodiment of having bipolar disorder. The illness can bombard and take over the mind of the individual.

Peace can seem as though it is in the far distant future. This disease is an illness that will challenge the peace and hope of the individual affected, as well as those closest to them. The behavior of some who have the illness can become unpredictable.

A sufferer's mood can range from great elation to deep sadness. When an individual is experiencing the wide range of moods from the illness, one's hope and peace of mind will be challenged. Peace of mind is not at the forefront when a bearer is in a depressed state.

I wholeheartedly believe that reading, studying, and meditating on the Word of God gave me peace of mind. My peace of mind was not sudden. It did not happen in a week or even months.

In fact, it took years of battling the disorder before I was able to obtain the coveted peace of mind. My suggestion for individuals who are in the midst of the various episodes of the illness is to never lose hope that you will acquire peace in your life. Meditating daily on the Word of God will gradually help the individual to develop inner peace.

Patience with oneself and the process of developing peace of mind is the key to obtaining it. Once a bearer of the disorder can obtain peace of mind, then they are on the road to recovery. Sometimes the road to recovery with anything in life can become a long and difficult process.

It is easy to lose patience and peace of mind when someone is recovering from a severe mental illness such as bipolar disorder. I believe that the individual who is committed to obtaining their peace of mind will receive it. Becoming closer to God through His Word is the first step to a mind of peace.

Social media has become an intricate part of our society and the world in which we live. In my opinion, it is both a blessing and a curse. Sure, there are some good things that happen as a result of it.

For example, when it is used correctly, it can benefit the user. Social media can help an individual reunite with friends, as well as long-lost relatives. Although these are positive examples of social media, there are also negative aspects of it that can affect one's mental health and peace of mind.

Unfortunately, there are some whose sole purpose and intent is to bully and tear down others that are participants of social media. Some of these negative individuals inflict harm upon others by their negative comments. This can affect people of all ages. When individuals post negative comments toward other members of social media, it can have a devastating effect on one's inner peace.

Personally, I do not partake in the use of social media because I know that a plethora of unfavorable posts or comments would affect me in a negative way. One might say that they tune out the unfavorable messages from negative social media users. Though this might be the case for a select few, I believe that the majority of the individuals on social media are curious about what others say.

Because of one's curiosity about what others might comment about them, this curiosity can lead to an individual's mental demise. Those who are at a relatively young age will become greatly affected and influenced about what their peers think about them. If an individual who is young receives an enormous amount of negative comments from so-called friends, that individual might lack the tools to overlook insults.

Video games and social media have had a significant effect on our society. Individuals whom are affected by this disorder and other mental illnesses should do all they can to preserve their hearts and minds. I am not saying that all individuals who experience mental illness should avoid all aspects of social media and the Internet.

What I am suggesting for individuals who are affected by the disease is that they should be both cognizant and careful in regard to the social media platform. A negative comment from someone on social media can derail an individual's journey to a peaceful life. Many who experience the illness have a heightened level of sensitivity.

Sufferers of the disorder might turn their anger inward as a result of bullying on social media. A depressive person cannot allow another individual to steal one's joy and happiness. This is why I suggest that an individual who is affected by the illness limit their social media intake and usage.

One cannot develop and sustain peace of mind with worrisome thoughts. Too much social media will lead the most positive individual to the loss of one's mind if they are not cautious. The individual who has the illness must learn one's symptoms and triggers. This could become the difference in maintaining and sustaining one's peace of mind. An individual's peace of mind will not consistently develop through the astronomical use of social media.

Inner peace can become extremely elusive particularly in the life of an individual with the illness. I can recall how I reacted when I received my initial diagnosis. My state of mind at that time was constant fear and confusion.

When an individual is journeying through life in a state of fear and confusion, that individual is on a dangerous path. One's mind should not be overloaded by chaos and turmoil. It will not function at its full potential when it is in that state.

As a result of a mind of confusion and turmoil, one's mental state will become affected. Our mind and thoughts are imperative in life. In the mind of all individuals on this earth, one can either think oneself well or become defeated by one's thoughts.

I am a firm believer that what we think in our mind will become a domino effect in regard to having peace of mind. If you think of beautiful and tranquil thoughts, I believe that it will affect one's overall mindset. It really does matter how we all think in our minds because having positive thoughts could one day be the difference in having a clear mind as opposed to having a confused mind.

Those affected by this disorder must learn how to develop inner peace in one's thoughts and mind. I am aware that it is not easy to obtain peace of mind when your thoughts are going a mile a minute. Some who are affected have made up in their mind that they will never acquire inner peace.

Peace in one's mind does not mean that one is void of struggles and problems. Society will have one to think that peace is obtained when an individual is trouble free. Many think that peace is when an individual is relaxing on a beach and free from all the cares in this world.

Realistically, every one cannot afford to take that dream vacation on a tropical island. Sometimes the individuals who can afford the expensive tropical getaways still do not have peace. They think that they will obtain peace externally.

We live in a world and society that is filled with facades. Some think that the only way they will have inner peace is by seeking things outwardly. For example, seeking peace externally through other people can lead to disappointment and frustration.

Peace from within begins and ends with one's mind and thoughts. Each individual must take an honest approach to one's life. No one can acquire and maintain peace of mind when they are in self-denial and not honest with oneself.

In my opinion, individuals who have the illness can think themselves well in the mind. If the individual has faith and hope that their condition will improve, then the bearer will have the peace of mind that they longed for. In order to develop peace of mind consistently, the individual must overcome the negative thoughts that can plague anyone.

There are choices that we all make each day. One can choose to strive for the peace that comes from within or remain in a confused state. Those affected by the disorder can honestly develop peace of mind when they approach it honestly and with vigor.

There are many that live a life of constant worry. Some worry about minute things in life. With the state of our world and society, it is understandable how one can have anxiety over the most normal activities.

Because of the uncertainty of catastrophic events that plague the world and society of today, many are living in fear. In many cases, unforeseen negative events are out of our control. We are living in a world that is filled with peril.

It seems as though the dangerous times are here to stay. Due to the perilous times in which we live, many are succumbing to fear and anxiety. A worry-filled life has become the norm for a plethora of people in this society.

No one can fully control the events that will occur in this world. Situations and circumstances are unpredictable. With the unpredictability of events, an individual could have a great amount of fear and worry.

Depressive persons must strive to live a life free of fear and worry. The goal of the mood of each individual with the illness should be an even keel mindset. One way of accomplishing the goal of a life free of worry is to take the one-day-at-a-time approach to life.

When I adopted this approach to life, I commenced to develop peace of mind. Though the world and society is riddled with crime and other negative occurrences, one can still maintain inner peace. Maintaining inner peace in one's mind can become difficult to sustain when turmoil is continuously present.

I compare the life of the individual with peace of mind to a tree that has endured all of the natural elements of the weather. In regard to the weather, there are enormous storms that the tree must endure throughout the various seasons in a given year. Although the tree might encounter great storms, the tree that is standing in the midst of the storm will prosper.

Those who are affected by bipolar disorder can use the example of a long-standing tree as an example of how to endure peace in the midst of chaos. In my opinion, the individual who is filled with anxiety and worry does not have the right mindset and approach to issues and problems. Some who are in constant worry are focused more on the problem rather than the lesson or positive outcome that can develop.

Individuals who worry constantly are not aware that they are living also in continuous sin. Our heavenly Father does not like His children to live in fear and worry. Those that worry is unintentionally trying to carry the weight of the world.

As mere humans, it can become a heavy burden to live a life of fear, worry, and anxiety. No one in this life can endure the storms of life without help. Sadly, there are some who may not have the support from friends and relatives. This is why it is imperative that all individuals affected by this disorder view themselves as resilient like the tree that is still standing.

Life can become cruel at times. Some do not have the luxury of living a peace-filled life. Many who have the illness may have a plethora of setbacks as a result of the disorder. It might become difficult for a sufferer to enjoy peace of mind when the symptoms and triggers of the illness are constant.

At the time that I was diagnosed with the disorder, I could not receive any joy in my life. I must admit that during that dark period in my life, I thought that I did not have a purpose to live. Although I never tried to commit suicide, the thought crossed my mind at that time. I did not have the peace of mind to discover God's plan for me.

Happiness and joy are difficult to come by when an individual cannot discover one's purpose and meaning in this world. Life will pass you by when there are not any plans to succeed. I believe that an individual with the illness is succeeding in life when they discover their purpose, which can lead to peace of mind.

As one develops peace of mind in life, one should enjoy the journey along the way. A bearer must take the time to laugh. Yes, there are times in this life that we must become serious, but one must take the time to have fun.

There was a period in my life in which I was continuously serious throughout the better part of each day. I did not take the time to have laughter. I was unaware how being serious all the time would ultimately affect my internal peace. This attitude inevitably affected my mindset.

Individuals who have this disorder must make having a peace of mind a top priority. It is unhealthy to journey through life with just one mindset. Those who are affected by the illness should aspire to develop a healthy balance in life. This balance can influence one's peace of mind and overall mood.

When an individual can navigate through life with laughter and a peace of mind, it will not matter if it is raining or sunshine outside. Some say that a certain amount of laughter could affect the brain positively. In my opinion, a daily dose of laughter can become just as vital to a sufferer's overall health and mood over time.

I believe that laughter is just as important as breathing each day. We all must take breaths in order to live. Having laughter in one's life may not cure the illness, but it will help the individual's gradual mood development.

The mood of an individual with this disorder must become stabilized in order to achieve balance and inner peace. If you or someone you love is affected by the illness, take time to laugh. It can make a world of difference in overcoming the extreme sadness that can plague the affected person.

With the mayhem of society, many are not having peace of mind, as well as not becoming content. It is difficult to find laughter when the world is progressively worsening. Those that experience the severity of bipolar disorder can find the time to laugh again.

Previously, I discussed how worry affects one's psyche and peace of mind. I believe that some worry because of fear of failure. In life, one must never allow oneself to become fearful and timid.

In my own life, I have experienced some failures. For example, there were romantic relationships that failed for various reasons. Also, I experienced failure in jobs that I hoped would work out.

Although some of my experiences in life did not pan out for whatever reason, I still have the peace of mind that I tried. One can have peace of mind despite failure. I think that we can all find the lesson from not succeeding at times.

Sure, one can learn valuable lessons from failures. In regard to bipolar disorder, some who are affected view themselves as failures in life because they have a mental illness. Because of this mindset, some fail to try in life.

Due to this attitude and mindset, the individual's peace of mind will elude them. One way that a bearer can acquire inner peace is by focusing on past successes. Dwelling on past failures will hinder an individual's growth and peace.

The best way to overcome and defeat the symptoms and triggers of this severe mental illness is to never throw in the towel on oneself. One would be surprised how peace of mind will develop when one perseveres through the illness. Will peace of mind become difficult to obtain for the sufferer? Realistically, in some severe cases of the disorder, the mindset of some will not allow them to have a peaceful mind.

Some who are affected will believe that they are failures through no particular fault of their own. In some cases, the bearer might come from a long line of family members that were not diagnosed with the disorder. The chemical imbalance from the brain will significantly affect the individual's attitude and mindset especially when the illness is left untreated. This is why some who are undiagnosed will elect to divulge in drugs and alcohol in order to escape mentally. The individuals who are undiagnosed are unaware about what is happening to them from within their mind and thoughts.

If you or someone you love is affected with the illness, strive to seek peace of mind by persevering through the disorder. An individual who perseveres in life is successful and far from a failure. The depressed person will ultimately develop peace of mind by maintaining great mental health through a life of perseverance and consistency.

Individuals with the disease are just as deserving of peace of mind than those who do not have the illness. The negative stigma of the illness causes some affected individuals to view themselves as unworthy. I have never heard of an individual having healthy peace of mind and self-esteem through feelings of unworthiness and failure.

Individuals with the disorder must find the courage and strength to persevere in spite of the illness. For some, there will be days of pain, as well as days of exuberant elation. The goal for every depressive person should be to focus on overcoming the disorder instead of dwelling on the negative thoughts of being a failure. When an affected individual can overcome the disorder through perseverance, then inner peace and peace of mind is on the horizon.

It is imperative that individuals who have bipolar disorder develop a daily routine. I believe that a daily routine will add structure to one's life. Also, daily routines can help with an individual's peace of mind.

My life has blossomed due to having structured tasks. I have been on a daily routine for several years. Everyone will not benefit from the same daily routine. What might work for one individual may not work or be beneficial to someone else.

Those affected with the illness must strive for structure in their lives. When a daily task is completed, it helps the individual who completed the task to have a sense of accomplishment. The completed and structured task will help with one's psyche.

I can recall how I felt when I was in school, and I was given a task to complete from my instructor. We all have been in school and had to complete an assignment that was due. Some chose to procrastinate and wait until the last night to complete the work.

Do you think that the individual who waited until the last moment to complete their assignment had peace of mind? Of course, that individual did not have genuine peace of mind from the due assignment because they did not develop a daily routine leading up to the completion of the assignment. The individual would have had peace of mind if they started working on the assignment each day instead of trying to cramp the completion of the assignment the night before it was due.

Developing a consistent daily routine for the bearer is imperative. The individual's overall mental health will improve when one has a daily regimen. The completion of regular tasks will give the individual both peace of mind and newfound confidence.

The daily routine that I commence with each day is prayer. There is not a day that goes by that I do not converse with the Creator. I have peace of mind that God will hear my prayers and requests.

It would greatly affect me if I deviated from my daily routine of prayer each morning. After I wash my face and brush my teeth, I talk with the heavenly Father. I would feel uncomfortable throughout the day by not beginning the day with God.

My peace of mind is sustained by conversing with God Almighty. There was a time in my life that I only talked with God before I went to bed. This was when I was in high school.

As I have matured in life, I realized that I had to seek a meaningful and sincere relationship with God and His Son in order to maintain peace. I knew that something had to change in my daily routine in order to maintain mental wellness. It does not require a great deal of effort to incorporate the Most High in one's daily regimen.

Besides conversing with God each morning, daily activities such as exercise and household tasks can also give an individual a mind of peace. These activities can help the individual with the peace of mind that the activity was completed. A sufferer has a greater chance of continuous wellness when they incorporate a daily routine in one's life.

Some chose to meditate to help them through troubles and problems. I believe that meditation is extremely vital in the life of the individual affected with the disorder. Meditating on the Word of God has been the key to my consistent mental wellness.

There are verses in the Word of God that can help an individual with anxiety. When these verses of Scripture are embedded in one's mind, I am certain that the individual will develop peace of mind eventually. The depressive person must have faith that meditating on God's Word will improve one's condition.

Not only does meditating on the Word of God help the individual with bipolar disorder with overall improvement, but also having a consistent prayer life can help anyone regardless of the illness that might affect them. I believe that praying multiple times within a day has significantly improved my peace of mind. Praying to the almighty God and His Son, Jesus, should not be treated like a magical request.

God may not improve one's condition instantaneously. The heavenly Father and His Son work on their own timetable. It might take some time for the bearer to acquire immediate results of peace of mind through prayer.

We live in a society and world that is always testing an individual's inner peace. There are many that believe that having a relationship with a friend or significant other will equate to a peaceful mind. In fact, I believe that the opposite is true.

No other human being can give the kind of peace that God can. Prayer is the way that we all communicate with the Creator and the blessed Savior. Unlike doctors, friends, family, and significant others, God and Jesus are there for all who call upon them.

A sufferer of bipolar disorder cannot go wrong by having daily prayer and meditation in one's life. Each affected person must find the time to have quietness and stillness at sometime within a day. This quietness and stillness can only be obtained through prayer and meditation.

Although some are not able to have quiet time in their homes due to having a plethora of occupants, the bearer must persevere in their quest to obtain a specific time that is void of noise and distractions. In regard to prayer and meditation, it can still occur in the midst of busyness and chaos. It is imperative that those who are bipolar learn how to consistently pray and mediate because it can help with the symptoms and triggers of the disorder.

Meditation and prayer is extremely beneficial to all who are affected by this severe mental illness. It can help the individual clear their mind from negative thoughts. As a sufferer, I have confirmation that daily prayer and meditation has gradually improved my mental mindset of peace despite ongoing negative world events.

Peace of mind is a state of mind that can become difficult to obtain in a violent and unpredictable world. The mind and heart are simultaneously working for peace. An active life of meditation and prayer will help each individual affected with the disease to gradually develop the peace of mind that they are hoping for.

The individual with bipolar disorder can overcome the illness when they learn how to mentally develop peace within their mind and heart. It is not a simple illness that can be overcome easily. Inner peace is something that many struggle with in life, including those individuals who are nonbearers.

Hopefully, in this chapter, the individual who might be affected by this illness can understand the process of maintaining, as well as sustaining one's peace of mind. Peace of mind and contentment in the mind of the sufferer can become difficult to acquire when the environment and world is in utter chaos. I am a firm believer that there is always hope for even the most severe case of the illness.

All who experience the illness must learn how to approach each day with anticipation. This mindset can become difficult for the individual who is in a depressed mood and state. When an individual is depressed, there is not anything to look forward to.

I can recall how I felt when I was deeply depressed. At that time in my life, I did not envision that I would have a life of joy and anticipation. After some time elapsed in my life, I realized that joy, inner peace, and peace of mind are not found externally through people, places, and things.

My joy and inner peace developed at its own gradual pace. Those affected by the disease must somehow find the strength and hope that peace will eventually come in one's mind. One will not obtain peace and contentment by concentrating on the external things in this world, which are, in many cases, out of one's control.

As members of this world and society, the only thing that we can do is do our best each day. If one can have the satisfaction that they gave their all, then that individual will acquire the desired peace from within. Bipolar disorder will never give the individual a mind of peace as long as the individual does not tackle it wholeheartedly.

Although each bearer of the disorder will not share the same experiences, it is imperative that each bearer does not allow the disorder to steal one's desire for peace, joy, and contentment. The goal of acquiring and maintaining inner peace does not have to elude the depressive person's life. It can only be obtained by a plethora of determination and an enormous amount of perseverance.

Peace of mind is not normal for those who are experiencing the illness. In fact, because some who are affected by the disease lack peace, some succumb to suicide. Each individual with the illness must learn how to cope with the illness before it gets to the stage of taking one's own life.

Some who experience the illness can overcome the illness by having the inner peace and peace of mind to combat it and defeat it. Time and patience are essential to the development of peace in regard to having the illness. One can gradually have peace in one's life in spite of having a disorder that affects the mind.

CHAPTER 5

The Battle Could Affect Those around You

F amily members of individuals with bipolar disorder are also affected by the illness. It takes extreme courage and strength to stand by bearers of the disorder. This illness requires love and patience from the individual's family.

The individual who is experiencing bipolar disorder requires a great amount of support from loved ones. It is an illness that can be overcome when the individual is aware that someone is in one's corner. Dealing with the symptoms of the disorder can be quite overwhelming for those closest to the sufferer.

I can recall how difficult it was for my mother when I was initially diagnosed with the illness as a teenager. There were times in which the disorder was getting the best of me. I was experiencing extreme moods due to the illness.

During that time of my extreme moods, my mother probably felt discouraged. When the onset of the illness initially occurred, I can recall the look on her face. I am certain that she felt helpless because there was not anything that she could have done. I needed the help of a professional.

Before I was diagnosed with bipolar disorder, my mother and I had a good mother-son relationship. She was blindsided when I displayed the symptoms of the disorder. I could imagine how difficult it was for her to receive the news that I was suffering from a mental disorder.

Fortunately, my mother was receptive of my diagnosis as opposed to my initial denial of the illness. Bipolar disorder affected my mother and I for several years before the disorder commenced to become under control. There was one particular time that I can recall how the illness affected my mother at her job.

Because of the severity of the episodes that I experienced due to the illness, my mother chose to take time off from work in order to help me cope with the symptoms of the disorder. She never told me, but in hindsight, I know how concerned she was with my mental health each day when she left to go to work. Due to the severity and unpredictability of the illness, I am certain that the illness also affected my mother internally.

Although she did not express it to me, I am certain that the illness can become a bit of a burden to loved ones of a depressive person. If the symptoms and triggers of the disorder are not treated professionally and properly, the unpredictability of this severe mental illness could divide a family. Though the bearer is experiencing the illness firsthand, the individual's loved ones are also experiencing it.

It is not the fault of the individual who has the disorder. Those with the illness must commend loved ones who are willing to also tackle the illness head on. Family members and loved ones of the sufferer, though affected by the disorder, will reap the benefits when the bearer is able to combat and overcome the disease.

Although some friends and loved ones may not experience having a mental illness, I am certain that the individual affected will welcome genuine love and empathy. Those who are closest to the bearer should aspire to understand the illness from the sufferer's perspective. Today, there is an enormous amount of information about the disorder.

Individuals who support the individual should not give up on them. I personally understand that it can become difficult to love and support some who bear the illness especially when the individual displays extreme mood swings. There may be times in which the depressive person might say unpleasant things.

For the majority of bearers of the illness, it could be the result of the chemical imbalance in one's brain that may cause the individual to lash out. The individual with the disorder must be loved unconditionally. They have to be reassured that those closest to them will not abandon them.

It can become difficult for the friends and loved ones of a bearer to persevere in the midst of an unpredictable episode. Patience and love are definitely required in the support of individuals suffering from the illness. The individuals who are supporting the individual with the disease may also need love and support from others at times.

For several years, I have experienced resurgence in my overall mental health. I must admit that I am prospering because I am healthy mentally. One of the reasons that I am enjoying prosperity in regard to my overall mental wellness is due to the love, patience, and support from my mother.

She has been supportive of my overall mental health from the beginning. When I revert back to how my behavior was in the past due to my illness, I can honestly see how difficult it must have been for one individual to support someone with bipolar disorder alone. I am reaping the benefits of mental wellness today because of her willingness to support me with her motherly and unconditional love.

Because of my mother's love and perseverance through the most challenging times from this disorder, I am now enjoying the benefits from her support. I have been consistent in my mental health because I have at least one supportive loved one. If you are supporting an individual with bipolar disorder, strive to continuously demonstrate love and perseverance toward him or her.

By exhibiting these qualities, the individual who is supporting the depressive person will inadvertently contribute to mental wholeness and wellness in their life. In order to experience improvement of the disorder, the individual must have love and support. Love and support does not necessarily have to come from a family member. A supportive friend can also suffice.

In regard to someone overcoming the valleys of bipolar disorder, it is imperative that the sufferer experience unconditional love from a friend or loved one. The support system of at least one person can help the bearer's improvement. I am certain that the individual with the illness will appreciate the perseverance and unconditional love from a supportive friend or loved one in the long run.

Impatience and frustration can become prevalent in those who are closest to the bearer of the illness. As a depressive person myself, I can empathize with how difficult that a sufferer can become.

A nonbearer of the disorder may not understand that the bearer of the disorder requires a substantial amount of time and attention. At the most challenging time that I was dealing with the illness, I was fortunate to have my closest relative supporting me. The depressive person can become quite a handful.

The behavior of an individual affected by bipolar disorder can become overwhelming to those who deal with the individual on a daily basis. Some may not be able to relate to the bearer of the illness. It can become an unbearable task for friends and loved ones to accept some of the high and low moods of the depressive individual.

There was a time when I was experiencing the symptoms of the illness, and I wanted someone to understand the illness from my perspective. During the most difficult time that I was experiencing the disorder, I tried desperately to communicate my feelings toward those individuals in my inner circle. Many of the friends and associates that I had at that time in my life could not understand the illness.

Because they did not understand that, I isolated myself from them. Due to an extreme mood of sadness and depression, they became incapable of empathy. Individuals who are dealing with the extreme moods of the disorder would like nothing more but to have family, friends, and loved ones to understand where they are coming from.

I am aware that the individuals who I surrounded myself with during that time in my life never interacted with an individual experiencing the disease. For many of my friends and associates, they did not have any inkling of what I was going through in my mind. When I was not my usual fun-loving self, I could imagine how odd it must have been for them to see me in another mood.

Some of the individuals whom I considered friends before the genesis of my illness commenced to gossip and say that I "lost it" because of my extreme behavior that I was exhibiting at that time. I can recall how hurt I felt when the individuals who I thought were my dear friends commenced to ostracize and exclude me. It is extremely disappointing and painful when those closest to the depressive person demonstrate great apathy.

Bearers of any illness need love and understanding from those who consider themselves close to the bearer. Instead of distancing oneself from an individual who is depressive, one should draw near to the sufferer. There are many things in life that one might find peculiar due to ignorance.

Anyone can fall victim to any illness at any given time in one's life. Although one might not understand the illness of a depressive person, it is imperative that the so-called friend or loved one of the bearer takes the time to empathize and understand. The bearer of the illness will appreciate the effort.

Many have heard that the first step to solving a problem is admitting that you have one. It is common for the family and loved ones of the individual diagnosed with a mental illness to dismiss it. We all would like to aspire to have great health, but it is unrealistic for those closest to the individual with a serious mental illness such as bipolar disorder to not admit to having it.

There was a time that I was ashamed of having the disorder. Those whom I was closest to at the time of my diagnosis could not fathom that I suffered from the disease. I can revert to an event some time ago that I attended in which my friends saw me taking psychiatric medicine.

When they asked me why I was taking medicine, I admitted to them that I had bipolar disorder. I can still vividly see the reaction on their faces when I told them that I had a mental condition. After I revealed my diagnosis to them, my friends commenced to respond in total denial.

Because my friends at the time reacted to the news of me having a mental illness by not embracing the information, I also began to put my condition on the backburner. Those who are affected with a psychiatric disorder should never disregard it. The bearer will experience more harm than good when friends and loved ones do not own the fact that an individual has the disease.

It is extremely difficult to accept that someone you love can be affected by a mental disorder. Some still view the psychological condition of bipolar disorder in a negative light. Therefore, individuals with this perspective will not accept that an individual whom they are fond of may need assistance from a licensed professional.

In my opinion, the family and friends of an individual who is diagnosed with the disorder can compound the illness to a greater extreme by denying it. When it comes to a severe psychological disorder, it must not become swept under the rug. This condition is extremely dangerous to the depressive person when left untreated.

An example of a family living in denial of the illness is when the doctor prescribes medication, and the family of the sufferer wrongly advises the individual not to take it. The family of the individual with the illness might have hope that their loved one could find another alternative. In many cases, a family that refuses to see that their loved one is in dire need of help is no better than a stranger on the street.

Denial is the number one hindrance to the individual who is affected by mental illness. Whether it is from the individual with the condition or those closest to the bearer, this attitude and mindset must be taken seriously. The shame and guilt that society places on those with mental conditions are attributed to the negative denial of some.

As a result of those with denial, the individual who has the disorder is robbed of improving one's mental health. Once the symptoms and triggers are identified, progress can be made. This will not happen if the family of the depressive person chooses to look the other way.

The friends and relatives who are accepting of the individual with the disorder must become extremely observant of the depressive person's behavior. Some who are experiencing the illness may not be aware of their actions. This is why it is imperative that the bearer of the disease has a reliable support system.

A trusted support system does not have to be enormous. It should consist of individuals who truly care for the sufferer. The members of a trusted support system should not only be observant but honest with the individual with the mental condition.

Individuals who take on the responsibility of support for the depressive person must also be committed to the mental health and overall care of the individual. The supportive person should not be too lax or overbearing toward the bearer. If the individual who is affected by the disorder feels pressure from members of the support system, it might affect the individual's progress.

Those closest to the individual affected by bipolar disorder must strive to recognize the triggers of the illness. For example, it is imperative that the individual who suffers from the disorder get an adequate amount of rest. Some who have the illness do not make sleep a priority.

Sleep is extremely beneficial to the individual with the disorder. Without a sufficient amount of rest, the cognitive decisions of the individual will become clouded. Although acquiring the proper amount of rest is vital to those who are not affected by the disorder, it is extremely imperative to the individual with the illness.

I can vividly remember how I would not receive the adequate amount of rest before my initial diagnosis. School and work were more of a priority for me than rest. I went to school for approximately five to six hours, then I would work an eight-hour evening shift. During that time, I did not have a car, so I would ride the bus.

There were some nights that I did not return home until twelve to one o'clock in the morning. I would have to eat a meal, then wake up at five in the morning to begin another day. I was unaware at that time that living each day in that fashion would eventually affect my mental health.

Also, I would not rest on the weekends during that time in my life because I was too busy going out and partying. This lifestyle of insufficient rest occurred approximately two years. After becoming diagnosed with bipolar disorder, the member of my support system, which was my mother, recognized that sleep was important to the recovery of my condition.

Sleepless nights are one of the symptoms that could trigger a manic episode of the disorder. Because this illness is an illness that affects the mind and brain, it is imperative that those closest to the individual observe the symptoms and triggers of the individual with the disorder. A well-meaning individual(s) of a supportive support system will recognize the individual's triggers.

In my opinion, individuals with bipolar disorder should not be pitied. The friends and loved ones of the bearer should treat the individual as normal as possible. It will benefit the sufferer when there is normalcy.

Previously, I mentioned that the individual who bears the disorder is not the disease itself. In fact, no one is the illness. It is just an illness that the individual just happens to have. This is why it is imperative that those closest to the individual who is affected with the disorder does not demonstrate any partiality toward the depressive person.

There are some who are close to those affected by mental illness that become advocates for the mentally ill. Some advocates might have had a friend or close relative that ultimately succumbed to the disorder. Due to the hurt and pain that the illness might have caused, the advocate might choose to lend one's money and time to nonprofit organizations that specialize in mental wellness.

Individuals with mental illness in past decades are not the forgotten. Today, there has been an improvement in the compassion of others who are not affected by psychological disorders. Due to the increase of individuals with these illnesses in our world and society, many have learned how empathy and care are welcomed to those who are experiencing disorders of the mind.

An increase in suicide in many countries around the world has forced many to take an in depth look at the individuals who are experiencing mental illnesses, such as, bipolar disorder. When I was growing up in the 1980s, it was taboo to talk about an individual with a psychiatric condition. The majority of individuals with a mental disorder were stereotyped as being lunatics.

Because of the negative stigma of mental illness during that time, some families chose to take a blind eye toward family members with a psychological disorder. Instead of some families being aggressive and proactive in the treatment of a loved one experiencing mental illness, some family members did not discuss the illness amongst themselves and others. Having compassion toward the depressive family member was ultimately substituted for shame and pity.

As an individual who has dealt with mental illness for several years, I believe that instead of someone feeling sorry for the mentally ill, it is more beneficial to demonstrate compassion and encouragement. Individuals with mental illness must learn how to encourage oneself. This can be achieved when those closest to the individual with the disorder have an environment of compassion and positive reinforcement.

Those who are affected by psychological illnesses must learn their value as a contributing member of society. When the individual affected by this disorder acquires self-love and self-worth, then there will not be any need to become pitied by those who are closest to the bearer, as well as others. The family and friends of the depressive person can make a world of difference when love and compassion is displayed instead of pity, which can lead to the demise of the individual with the condition.

Those who are dealing with a friend or loved one that has bipolar disorder have an enormous task of supporting the individual with the disorder. Sometimes the ones who are caring for the depressive person might miss out on one's interest. Caring and supporting an individual who is affected with this mental illness can at times become difficult to bear.

Some who are in close contact with the bearer of the illness may not have the time to experience and enjoy fun activities. These unsung heroes may feel obligated to put the wants and needs of the depressive person first. Many of the individuals who care and support the individual with the disorder do it out of love.

In many cases, the friends and loved ones of the individual affected suppress their own interests and desires in order to accommodate the needs of the bearer of the disorder. The individual(s) who support the individual with the illness must be careful that they are not consumed and overwhelmed. Previously, I mentioned how imperative it is for those who are caring for the affected individual to have and maintain balance in one's life.

Though I have experienced the disorder firsthand, I now recognize that it is vital to the friends and loved ones of the individual affected by this mental condition to take time to do activities in which they enjoy. Because this particular illness can become extremely intense, those who are supporting the depressive person must make it a priority not to lose themselves. If the friends and loved ones of the individual with bipolar disorder do not take the time to care for oneself, then they will not be any good for the individual experiencing the disease.

I can recall how I had a doctor who was consumed with the care of my illness. When I initially seen this particular doctor, we had a normal doctor-patient relationship. After some time had passed, our professional relationship commenced to take on a relationship like that of a family.

There were times when the illness was so severe that this doctor took on the role of a close family member. It was refreshing for me that a doctor would take a personal interest in my condition. In regard to this particular doctor, I could tell that my struggles with the disorder at that time also became consuming.

I believe that this doctor cared so much for my overall mental wellness that my condition commenced to have a consuming effect on the doctor. If a doctor can become overwhelmed by this particular disorder, then the family and friends of the individual affected could also become easily overwhelmed. Bipolar disorder is an illness that must be attacked with care and empathy.

I must admit that my condition improved because of the care and concern from my doctor during that time, along with my closest relative. With the severity of the disorder, I can understand how those who are closest to the depressive person could become overbearing. Hopefully, the individual with the condition can become grateful and thankful of the sacrifices and concern of those who care.

Close friends and relatives of the individual who is affected with the disorder must never lose hope and patience that the depressive person can overcome the illness. I believe that the depressive person has a greater chance of relinquishing the stronghold of the disease when those closest to the individual do not give up on them. The worst scenario that an individual who is affected by mental illness can have is a situation in which a family member or dear friend is unwilling to persevere in the journey toward mental wellness and wholeness.

In order for the individual with the disorder to have a successful outcome in life, in spite of being diagnosed with a severe mental illness, it is by having the affected individual and those closest to the bearer commit to therapy. Therapy from a licensed psychiatrist can help the depressive individual, as well as loved ones become better equipped with patience. It is a continuous process for both the individual with the illness and the depressive person's loved ones.

Bipolar disorder is an illness that requires patience. The bearer of this disorder does not have a chance of overcoming it without patience and perseverance from the individual's friends and relatives. I understand that at times it may become difficult to exercise patience toward an individual who might be behaving irrationally.

My victory in overcoming the disorder did not happen immediately. There were countless hours of therapy that my mother and I experienced. In my opinion, a family that pays their dues in therapy could have hope for the future as a result of it.

Some families that are dealing with the individual with the psychological disorder dread going to therapy. Unfortunately, there are friends and loved ones that do not feel that talking with a doctor on a consistent basis could help develop tolerance for the individual with the mental condition. Committing to therapy for a significant amount of time takes a plethora of courage and perseverance from the loved ones of the individual bearing the disorder.

The goal for all involved in the treatment of the individual with the psychological disorder is for the individual to function at a reasonable level in society. This specific goal is never accomplished in haste. It will require months or even years of intense therapy in order for an individual with severe mental illness to improve and thrive in a dog eat dog world.

In my personal battle with the disorder, I believe that therapy helped my mother to acquire patience with the illness. The illness is never the core of the depressive individual. It is the result of the symptoms.

If one is dealing with an individual with a mental disorder, my suggestion is to strive to obtain patience. Patience with the bearer could potentially improve the individual's condition significantly. Therapy and patience are two of the ways that the loved ones of the individual with the psychological illness can cope with the stresses of the disorder.

The individual living with this severe mental illness are only as good as the individual(s) that love and care for the bearer. If those closest to the individual with bipolar disorder are not optimistic, then there is a greater chance that the individual affected with the illness will not attack the illness in a positive mindset. Each sufferer of the disorder should be aware that those closest to him and her would demonstrate unconditional love toward them.

Some who are bearers of the disorder do not have the luxury of being surrounded by a loving family. When the depressive person has to take on the illness, as well as a nonsupportive family, it can become a recipe for the illness worsening. It can become more burdensome for the affected individual when the relatives of the bearer decide to allow that individual to face the illness alone.

A depressive person is only as good as those closest to them. The majority of individuals who are affected by bipolar disorder might not realize the value of a nonjudgmental friend or family member. We live in a society in which many unfairly judge its members. There is not any pleasure for anyone being judged.

I can imagine the mindset of the individual who feels judged by those closest to them for having a mental condition. Whether or not one is a bearer or nonbearer of a psychological disorder, we all must have someone in our life that will vouch for us. Those who are affected by mental illness need an additional amount of love and support from a loving support system.

How can an individual who is affected by a significant mental illness improve? I believe that the friends and loved ones of the depressive person hold the key to overall improvement of the condition. In my experience in having the disorder, I became aware that the only way that I would conquer this disorder was by surrounding myself around optimistic individuals. Also, I made a conscious decision to love those pessimistic friends and loved ones from afar.

Close friends and loved ones of the depressive individual must be commended for their willingness to persevere with the individual in spite of the negative murmurings that being associated with an individual with a mental illness may bring. Although the stigma of someone having a psychological disorder has become less of an issue in recent years, it is still an illness that some still cannot accept. Those closest to an individual experiencing mental illness are considered special when they continue to support the individual throughout difficult trials as a result of the disorder.

Dealing with an individual affected by a psychological condition can prove difficult. It takes an extraordinary person to persevere and support the individual with the illness. This is because the condition can become quite unpredictable within the depressive person. Those who choose to continually love and support the individual with the disorder, whom could potentially display extreme mood swings, might not realize how vital support can become in helping the individual with their mental health.

Loved ones and close friends of the individual who is affected by the illness must not lose hope. I am a firm believer in the impossible. There are some illnesses that have a grim prognosis for improvement.

In the case of the bearer of a psychological illness such as bipolar disorder, the individual's family will have greater success in the treatment of the illness when the family commits to mental wellness. As a result of a family's commitment to achieving success in overcoming the disorder, their loved one has a chance to defy the odds. Family and friends of an individual dealing with a mental condition cannot 100 percent become assured that the individual experiencing the condition will live a prosperous and successful life.

The majority of individuals with severe mental illness will have a lifelong duration of being monitored by a psychiatrist. Not only does the doctor monitor the progress of the illness, but the family of the depressive person also monitors the condition. Relatives of the individual with the disorder have more insight into the daily dealings of the individual affected.

When I was experiencing some of the negative symptoms of the illness, there were certain behaviors that I did not recognize within myself. During that time, I could not observe my own triggers. It took the observation and monitoring from my close relative to convey the behavior and symptoms of the illness to the doctor.

Those who care and support the individual with the disorder are the eyes and ears to the doctor. This is why it is imperative for the individual with the condition to have a reliable support system. There might be times in which the bearer of the illness cannot express his or herself.

In some instances, an alert family member or loved one could be the only way that the doctor can determine how to treat their patient. Loving and supporting a depressive person can become both overwhelming and time-consuming. With hope, patience, and prayer, the loved ones of the individual with the disease can reap the benefits of their love and sacrifice.

I believe that the family and loved ones of the bearer of the illness see the results of their patience and sacrifice when the bearer is able to recognize their own triggers of the disorder, as well as becoming a valued member of society. This can only occur when the loved one or close relative is invested in the care and the improvement of the sufferer. The family and close relatives of the individual with the severe mental disorder can rest more easily if their loved one is able to overcome the condition.

As I previously stated, many say that there is not any cure for bipolar disorder. It is easy to lose hope when the clinical prognosis does not look promising. The only way that an individual with the illness can anticipate hope and success in life despite having a negative mental condition is through the tireless support from caring friends and relatives.

CHAPTER 6

One Must Refrain from Illegal and Mind-Altering Substances

Today, we live in a culture in which drugs and other mood-altering substances are prevalent. The alcohol and drug epidemic has gotten increasingly worse in our society. Because of the commonality of the problem, government officials have no choice but to address the issue.

There are millions of young people who are affected by the use of substances that have a negative effect on one's mind. Some who partake in the use of mind-altering substances do not realize how dramatically these substances can alter the brain. Many users are only concerned with the immediate result of "getting high."

Those who are affected by bipolar disorder should not entertain using substances such as alcohol and illegal drugs. It can prove to become a dangerous and deadly combination. When an individual who has the disorder decides to use these substances, they are unaware that the symptoms of the illness are elevated.

For example, an individual who is contemplating taking one's own life will more likely carry out that plan after indulging in drug usage. The issues and symptoms of the individual with the illness do not disappear when the bearer wants to escape. Sadly, in some instances, some who are mentally ill who participate in the use of illegal and mind-altering substances disregard how imperative it is to the improvement of one's mental condition to have a clear mind.

An individual who is affected by a psychological disorder must demonstrate great restraint when those around the individual with the mental condition are using mind-altering substances. It requires an enormous amount of self-discipline for the bearer of the disorder not to succumb to peer pressure. Although an individual is affected with a psychiatric condition, that individual in most cases still knows the difference between right and wrong.

In my opinion, an individual who has a psychological condition should do everything within their power to avoid drugs and alcohol. Previously, I discussed how vital it is for the depressive person to have a supportive support system. A supportive support system will consist of individuals who will have a positive influence on the bearer.

Individuals who truly care for the individual with the mental disorder will take that person's mental state into consideration. Individuals who are part of a reliable support system have the affected individual's best interest. This means that the individuals who support the depressive person will not endorse the use of substances that could mentally affect the individual with the psychological illness.

Each individual who has an illness that affects the mind must become cognizant of what they are putting into it. Bipolar disorder and the use of illegal and mind-altering substances should not have a place amongst the individual who is experiencing the disorder. One's clear mental state is more important than trying to obtain a break from reality.

Alcohol is a beverage that many consume worldwide. When it is consumed by adolescence whose brains are not fully developed, it can contribute to a whole host of problems. In my own life, I had a brief experience with the usage of alcohol.

I have been extremely forthcoming in regard to my consumption of alcohol when I was a late teen. My experience with alcohol commenced when I attended college. Although my alcoholic consumption lasted a short time in my opinion, I believe that it had an influence on my mental health.

Though I am not a licensed psychiatrist, when I revert back to the time before my initial diagnosis, I would consume alcohol on a regular basis. In fact, months after I decided not to partake in the use of alcohol, I was diagnosed with bipolar disorder. What I was doing during the time that I drank alcohol is what is commonly referred to now as binge drinking.

There were times that I would drink heavily throughout the weekend. During the weekdays, I would not indulge in alcoholic use because I was attending classes. As soon as Friday night came, I would go to the local drug store and purchase an alcoholic beverage.

After combining my depressed mood with binge drinking on the weekends, in hindsight, I can see how it affected my brain. I was not aware how binge drinking could affect me psychologically. Because I was a teen during the time of my extreme alcoholic use, I naively thought that I was invincible.

It took a morning in which I blacked out after a night of heavy drinking for me to realize that I had to refrain from that lifestyle. I believe that if I did not follow through with the decision to cease from binge drinking, the result could have been worse than the development of a psychiatric condition. Adolescence and young adults who participate in the usage of alcohol do not consider how detrimental it can become to one's brain and mental wellness.

Individuals who drink alcohol and use mind-altering substances do not consider the long-term effect that these substances have on one's mind and brain. I cannot speak on the behalf of all who are affected by this psychiatric disorder. Each individual affected by the illness has various experiences and circumstances.

I can only comment on my experience with the disease. Also, I do not know if I had not made the poor decision to indulge in alcohol, I would have experienced a psychological illness. What I do know is that the usage of alcohol and mind-altering substances can have a great influence over one's mental health and wellness over time.

The mind and brain of each individual really matters. If the individual who participates in the usage of alcohol and other substances elects to neglect their cognitive functions, then a mental illness might become a result. When an individual decides not to indulge in a lifestyle that includes mind-altering substances, that individual is wise.

One of the main reasons why I decided to engage in the use of alcohol was escapism. I thought that if I took a few hours to drink my problems away, I would be fine. This way of thinking eventually compounded my problems.

The worst thing that an individual can do if they feel depressed is to indulge in mood-altering substances. Our mind and brain are not meant for negative stimuli such as alcohol. Some are not aware how drinking can have a negative effect on one's mental wholeness in a matter of time.

Each individual who partakes in the use of mind-altering substances will have a variety of reactions. There are some who are not affected by these substances in comparison to others. For myself, indulging in alcohol, although for a brief period in my life, has affected my long-term mental health.

If I had known that trying to escape my problems through an intense weekend of binge drinking would lead me to being diagnosed with bipolar disorder, I would not have ever engaged in it. A few moments of escape from reality is not worth a lifetime of mental illness. I understand that drinking and the use of other substances are not the sole reasons why some are diagnosed with a psychiatric disorder, but in my opinion, it can contribute to the condition.

Self-medicating through the use of mind-altering substances is one of the culprits of some having a mental disorder. I can recall how I anticipated drinking alcohol, when I had spare time, in order to help me escape my feelings of loneliness and depression. This can become a dangerous state of mind to be in.

Many individuals who choose to self-medicate are unaware of the underlining issues that can develop as a result. Some who self-medicate through the use of indulging in mind-altering substances may not be aware of a family history of mental illness because the illness may have been dormant within the individual who was undiagnosed. In my experience with alcoholic usage, I was unaware that I had a family history of individuals who suffered from mental illness.

I am a native of New Orleans, Louisiana. Partying and drinking are a way of life for many of the locals. If an individual who resides in that city desires to engage in the use of mind-altering substances, it is easily and readily available.

In my family history, there is a long line of family members who chose to escape their issues through the use of alcohol and other substances. I believe that many of them wanted to escape their troubles by indulging in an unhealthy lifestyle. Engaging in a prolonged lifestyle of partying will affect one's mental health at some point.

It is foolish to think that one will not escape the consequences of an indulgent lifestyle. An individual who chooses to self-medicate is opening a Pandora's box of mental health issues. In the end, one's problems will still be there. Choosing to escape the issues that plague many in life cannot be overcome through a lifestyle of drinking and partying.

In our society, there are a plethora of distractions that can contribute to an individual having a mind of chaos and confusion. A wild and crazy lifestyle of drugs and alcohol usually leads to an individual having some form of depression and anxiety. I believe that many who are diagnosed with bipolar disorder might have had some experience with some type of mind-altering substances.

This disorder can become more difficult to tame when the bearer is under the influence of a substance. An individual who is affected by the illness must come to the realization that it is no longer prudent to engage in a partying lifestyle. Each depressive person should aspire to live healthy.

I am aware that living a lifestyle free of using substances that could affect one's mind can become difficult to obtain. Some develop an addiction to these mind-altering substances, which can affect one's mood. When someone is under the influence of any type of chemical, they are not cognizant about how it will also affect one's mood, mind, and behavior.

There are some who will continue to defy what their doctors suggest when they are diagnosed with a psychological disorder. In regard to the use of alcohol or any other type of chemical substances, I am certain that no viable doctor will approve and recommend the usage of these substances while taking psychotropic medicine. The medicine that a licensed psychiatrist prescribes is only meant to treat the mood and behavior of the affected person's current symptoms and condition.

An individual with bipolar disorder who is also affected by addiction must strive to listen to the doctor and other health care professionals who are treating them. It can become difficult for the bearer of the illness to become open to the suggestions of individuals who never had an issue with addiction or mental illness. A depressive individual who is struggling with addiction is usually familiar with a nonapologetic lifestyle in which anything goes.

Individuals who are diagnosed with a dual diagnosis of a psychiatric condition and addiction typically have an enormous battle to conquer. Many who are affected by these conditions must understand the importance of refraining from mind-altering substances. They must develop the mindset that chemical substances that can affect the mind are only polluting one's brain.

Hopefully, the individual who is bearing both diseases of mental illness and addiction can overcome the battle within the mind. Those who support the individual should understand the severity of these illnesses. It requires great courage, strength, and determination to combat these conditions.

Having a dual diagnosis of addition and bipolar disorder can become overwhelming. If the individual envisions a healthy lifestyle, one can combat it. In order to become successful in overcoming these conditions, the individual has to acquire a desire to defeat it.

I have seen personally how the use of alcohol and other mind-altering substances can alter an individual's personality. Those who use these substances do not consider how they are hurting themselves in all aspects of life. A problem arises when these chemicals commence to affect someone psychologically.

Individuals who are living with psychological disorders must strive to become disciplined. It does not benefit the depressive person when he or she chooses to live a life that is dependent on mind-altering chemicals. I am reminded of a commercial that ran years ago that coined the phrase, "A mind is a terrible thing to waste."

Participating in the use of alcohol and other substances essentially limits the mental growth of that individual. With the continued use of substances that affects the mind, the partaker of these substances is damaging their brain cells and cognitive awareness. Sometimes the mind can become unforgiving.

The mind is unforgiving when the individual's mental condition does not improve as a result of using chemical substances such as drugs and alcohol. An individual with prolonged use of substances that affect the mind and brain may never get back to being the person that they once were. This is just the reality of some who have mental illness, as well as addiction issues.

Bipolar disorder is a mental condition that is best attacked soberly. It may seem that the individual who is affected by the condition can have an occasional glass of wine or alcohol, but this is only a misconception. For some diagnosed with the illness, it might become an uphill battle to cease from drinking all together.

When I would drink alcohol before I was diagnosed for a short while, it had become my way of life. I did not view it as an issue when I would consume two forty-ounce alcoholic beverages in one night. Eventually, my drinking of these substances not only affected my personal relationship with my significant other at that time, but I did not have a clue that my usage would affect my mind, brain, and personality.

Although I did not go into a rehab facility for my abuse of alcohol, I must say that being diagnosed with bipolar disorder forced me to take a long look at the error of my ways during that time in my life. I was blessed and lucky enough not to allow the drinking to turn into a full-blown addiction. It was a blessing in disguise when the doctor revealed to me that I had to cease from drinking any type of alcoholic beverage.

In my opinion, individuals who use alcohol or any other type of mind-altering substances are only a shell of oneself. Though it is said that the use of alcohol brings out the individual's true self, as a former partaker, I disagree. For me, I was not my authentic self when I engaged in it.

The use of chemical substances that can cause an individual to have a psychiatric disorder must not be taken lightly. An individual who is influenced by these substances are never the core person inside. It is always best for the depressive and the addictive person to strive to become their authentic self without the influence of these substances.

There are some who are diagnosed with this severe mental illness that will march to the "beat of their own drum." Individuals who are affected by a psychological disorder such as bipolar disorder may naively trust one's own instincts. It is unwise to continue navigating through life in the same stagnant position.

Many who are affected with the disorder will continue to abuse alcohol and other substances despite the suggestion of a competent doctor. When a licensed psychiatrist suggests that their patient abstain from the usage of chemical substances, some depressive persons choose to become defiant. This is the wrong attitude to have when the doctor's suggestion is to refrain from the use of mind-altering substances that could change and do damage to one's life.

I have personally known individuals who are diagnosed with the condition who are stubborn and set in their ways. Those who have the disorder will disregard the sage advice of individuals who have the bearer's best interest in order to engage in the use of chemical substances. If the advice of experienced health professionals cannot penetrate the mind of the depressive person, then there might not be any hope in regard to another alternative.

Some who have the dual diagnosis of bipolar disorder and drug addiction may feel hopeless. Each individual who has these diagnoses can either react in two ways. They can number one have an apathetic attitude and succumb to the diseases, or they can choose to take the dosage of medicine as prescribed and cease from indulging in any form of substances that could negatively alter and affect the mind.

Individuals who combine chemical substances with psychiatric medication are sadly not a select few. It has become a widespread issue in this country when individuals who are affected with severe mental illness decide to nullify doctor's orders and take prescription medication with other substances. As a result of individuals abusing prescription medicine with other mind-altering substances, many who abuse the usage of these medicines with the combination of other substances are not respecting the process in overcoming the condition.

Bearers of the disorder must not take it upon oneself to combine one's medication with other substances that affects one cognitively. The majority of individuals who participate in prescription medicine abuse are oblivious to the power of these medicines. There is a reason why on the bottles of these medications, it has a caution.

Typically, the caution on the medicine bottle states that the use of the prescribed medicine can cause extreme drowsiness. Also, on these medication bottles, it warns the user to demonstrate great care when operating a motor vehicle. The combination of prescription medicine with even a small amount of alcohol could lead to the individual with a severe mental condition to exhibit a greater increase in psychosis.

The psychiatric medication that the doctor prescribes is meant to affect one's mood. There is not any need to add on to the medication by indulging in the use of other substances. Some underestimate the potency of these drugs.

Medication for bipolar disorder or any other psychological disorder usually requires taking medication that will help the individual with their behavior. I have learned from personal experience that it is imperative that the bearer of the illness takes one's medication. Although I never had an issue with taking prescribed psychotropic medicine with other mind-altering substances, I have always understood the significance of not combining prescribed medicines with other substances that could affect one's cognitive reasoning and decisions.

Prescription medicine is taken by millions all around the world. In the case of taking psychotropic medicine, I believe that if the individual with the mental condition takes the medicine as prescribed, the individual, as well as others, should see a difference in the individual's mood. The key to overcoming mood swings as a result of the illness is to refrain from other chemical substances that could alter the mind while taking the prescribed medicine.

It took some time for me to come into agreement with what my doctor and support system had been emphasizing all along. They all emphasized how taking the medicine as prescribed would positively help my mood. Though psychotropic medicine is vital to the depressive person's overall mental wellness and wholeness, the individual who is affected with the disorder must never become curious about the combination of prescribed medication and mind-altering substances.

In my opinion, the curiosity of combining mind-altering substances with medicines that are prescribed to alleviate symptoms of the disease is typically the bearer's downfall. Some who commit this error hopefully will not live a life of regret. Because the individual who is affected by the disorder becomes curious, it can also lead to a life of harm and pain.

My suggestion for individuals who are affected by bipolar disorder or any other mental illness is to never entertain one's curious thoughts about what it would be like to combine medication with other chemicals. An individual does more harm than good to oneself when they choose to journey on that dark path. If one has friends and associates who are applying pressure to engage in the mismanagement of one's psychotropic medicines, then try to find new friends who can respect you, as well as your condition.

Whether or not one realizes, misuse of drugs of any kind does not do anything to enhance one's life. A moment of euphoria from the combination of legitimate drugs and other substances is not worth the harm, pain, and disappointment that it could potentially cause. Curiosity must never become a factor when taking prescribed psychiatric medication. The affected individual's mood will become negatively affected when an individual deviates from the prescribed dosage.

Individuals who are affected by severe mental illness must not allow alcohol and other substances to have precedence and priority in one's life. Those who are bearing the disorder should dare to be different. It takes a strong and courageous person to not succumb to the lure of mixing prescribed medicines with other substances.

Bipolar disorder can become a struggle to overcome. The individual with the disorder can make the condition worse by using other substances that affect the mind. It is extremely imperative that the depressive person has a support system around them that can make the bearer accountable.

Sufferers of the illness should welcome those who will not allow one to partake in activities that could negatively affect one's progress. The depressive person can become successful in combating the illness without the usage of mind-altering substances. In my opinion, I do not see how using mind-altering substances could positively help the individual become victorious in one's quest for mental wellness.

In our world and society of today, many are enduring a battle for their mental health. With the uncertainty of the world, I understand how easy it is to look for other outlets to escape the chaos. A sound mind is not promised with the gradual decline of our cities and neighborhoods.

Mental wellness and wholeness will not be obtained when an individual cannot abstain from the use of drugs and alcohol. Those who are affected by mental illness do not have to become a negative statistic. There are countless individuals with the disorder who overdose and die from drug misusage.

This is why it is imperative that an individual with the illness strive to take the initiative to refrain from additional substances that can affect one mentally. The individual should ask oneself about how using mind-altering substances contributes to one becoming a valued member of society.

There are only two outcomes that could result from an individual who is misusing one's medication and indulging in the use of other substances. One outcome is either going to jail or prison. The other outcome of misusage of psychotropic medicine with the use of drugs and alcohol is the grave.

Unfortunately, these two outcomes are a common problem that is plaguing the United States. Many promising young men and women are succumbing to this widespread prescription and mind-altering drug epidemic. Some who participate in the mismanagement of prescribed psychiatric medicines and chemical substances do not care enough about themselves to cease from engaging in it.

Acquiring enough courage to not partake in the misusage of prescribed psychiatric medicine and other mind-altering substances requires a plethora of will and self-discipline. This discipline can only be obtained when the depressive individual desires to have mental wholeness. It will require a team of support from family, friends, and the physician to develop the mental toughness to refrain from prescription medicine abuse.

Journeying through life without the aid of mind-altering substances such as drugs and alcohol will significantly benefit the individual who is affected with the disorder. When an individual has a psychological condition, it is imperative that the individual avoid the temptation of using those substances. A mind that is clear from the use of mind-altering substances can equate to a successful life.

I have been forthcoming in my brief time of indulging in alcohol. It was a time in my life that my brain was not fully developed. I believe that a full adult brain is not fully developed until that individual matures into their early to midtwenties.

During the time that I was engaging in alcoholic usage, I was a late teen. I am certain that bipolar disorder did not manifest itself prior to the alcohol abuse. Previously, I stated how some could have a family gene of mental illness.

There are some who are born with the mental illness gene that will never experience having a psychological episode. I firmly believe that in my case, the mental illness gene commenced to come into the forefront due to my bout with heavy drinking. Naively and unknowingly, I could have possibly accelerated my mental condition by participating in underage alcohol consumption.

If you the reader have bipolar disorder or you know someone with the condition, do not allow yourself or the bearer of the illness to indulge in the use of alcohol or any other mind-altering substance in your presence. By allowing the depressive person access to these substances, the nondepressive person is being an enabler to a bad habit. A real friend of the individual with the disorder will risk their friendship in order to help the individual remain on a straight path.

The brain of the individual with mental illness is significantly different from those who do not have the condition. Sufferers of mental illness will drastically impair their brains even more with continuous use of substances that are not meant for cognitive enhancement and growth. Individuals with severe mental illness do not have the luxury of participating in activities that have the potential of negatively impairing one's brain.

We all have only one mind and brain. Regardless if one has a psychological disorder or not, each individual should strive to be good to it. Indulging in alcohol and other substances only hinders the development of healthy cognitive activity.

There are numerous activities that an individual could partake in to stimulate the mind. Exercising and listening to good music of interest are activities that can help the brain thrive cognitively. These are healthy examples of fun activities that can be enjoyed without mind-altering chemicals.

As an individual who has experienced having a mental condition, I must say that there is more to life than drinking and using substances that affect the mind. Although it may sound cliché, it is more beneficial to get high on life the right way than getting high on substances that do not enhance one's psychological growth. The mind and brain responds positively when one feeds it with positive stimuli.

Medication that is intended to help an individual progress from the symptoms of a psychological disorder can sometimes lead to an accidental or unintentional death. It is imperative that the depressive person does not intentionally abuse the use of one's psychotropic medicine. Sadly, this is the case for many who are suffering from severe mental illness and suicidal thoughts.

As an individual who has overcome the stronghold of bipolar disorder, I can empathize and relate to the struggles of some who bear the illness. The feeling of hopelessness can become difficult to avoid in the midst of the disorder. The mistake that some make when interacting with an individual affected by the disease is thinking that the depressive person can magically get over the condition.

Those who are living with bipolar disorder must aspire to see the meaning and purpose of one's life. Life as an individual living with a severe mental illness can become difficult to journey through without love of oneself. Abusing psychiatric medicine with other substances is not the picture of self-love.

There are many who are affected by severe psychiatric conditions who do not view themselves as defeating the condition. Because of lost hope of the depressive individual, succumbing to the disorder by combining a cocktail of psychiatric medicine with mood-altering drugs seems like the likely result. For you the reader or anyone who feels that their only way to escape the hurt, pain, and disappointment of life is by ending it with medication and various substances, I am here to tell you that you can overcome the extreme hopelessness and sadness.

When I went through my period of sadness and darkness, I too almost gave up on life. One day, I decided that I was not going to allow my psychological disorder to dominate my life. Although I could have chosen a life of addiction, I knew that the disease of addiction does not have anything to do with happiness and mental wholeness.

In this chapter, I discussed how beneficial it could be to an individual who is affected with bipolar disorder or any other severe mental condition to strive for a life that is void of mind-altering substances. Also, I discussed how vital it is for the bearer of the illness to listen to the suggestions and recommendations of a viable and licensed psychiatrist to help in the battle to refrain from mind-altering substances with prescribed psychiatric medication. Individuals who are affected by psychological disorders such as bipolar disorder must find a healthy alternative in combating the condition.

I understand that life can become difficult within itself. It is extremely enticing to want to escape the pressures of life with the aid of other substances. Escaping from life can lead to an unwarranted death. The individual who is affected by the disorder must somehow establish a plan to not succumb to the condition by participating in activities that will enhance one's hope and desire to abstain from substances that negatively hinders one's mind.

CHAPTER 7

Get Proper Rest

Studies have shown that an adequate amount of sleep is vital. Sleep is just as important as eating at least three square meals within a day. There are some who do not give rest a top priority.

I used to be that person who did not value rest in my younger days. When I matured in life, I realized the importance of it. Individuals who are living with bipolar disorder must prioritize getting a sufficient amount of sleep.

Before I was initially diagnosed with the disorder, I lived an overly active life. My life consisted of school, work, and the club life. I was the type of individual who never wanted to stay at home.

In fact, I had plenty of late nights and early mornings. Ignorantly and naively, I did not consider during that time that lack of rest and sleep could contribute to both exhaustion and a mental breakdown. The mindset that I had at that time was sleep was for the weak and elderly.

Those who are living with a psychological disorder such as bipolar disorder must learn how to value rest. An individual in the manic phase of the disorder may also have little regard for sleep. The manic individual will want to accomplish so much in a given day that they do not realize that they are harming their brains by not sleeping and resting enough.

Proper rest is an ally to those who are in the midst of a manic episode. Individuals who are in a manic episode must become convinced that sleep and rest are key components in returning to a normal level. An individual who is manic must come to the realization that they cannot accomplish their tasks and goals without adequate and sufficient rest.

It is unrealistic for someone to think that they could accomplish all of their goals and tasks within a day. I understand that there may be days in which the tasks are completed. Though there might have deadlines for a specific task, rest and sleep should still have precedence in one's life.

Our heavenly Father rested on the seventh day. We as mere human beings should also set a time each day to rest. Without proper rest, an individual cannot thrive and prosper. Every living species on earth must rest and humans are no different.

A well-rested individual is vibrant. Those who are bearing a mental illness should incorporate rest and sleep into one's routine. If the depressive person can get the proper rest, then that individual will feel more rejuvenated.

As an individual who understands the psyche of being manic, I now know the importance of having enough rest. When I commenced to prioritize my rest, my condition improved dramatically. There is not anything wrong with trying to complete goals and tasks, but it is imperative that all individuals especially those who are experiencing a psychological condition give one's mind and brain proper rest.

Bipolar disorder is essentially a chemical imbalance in the brain. The individual who is experiencing the disorder must learn how beneficial that sleep can become to the overall improvement of the condition. Bearers of the illness should not take quality sleep time for granted.

When an individual is able to obtain a sufficient amount of sleep, it can help the individual with their mood. Though bipolar disorder is a result of an imbalanced brain, it is also a mood disorder. Let's face it. We are not ourselves mentally, physically, and emotionally when we are sleep deprived.

I believe that the common denominator to all of my experiences with manic episodes was due to a lack of sleep. Sure, I accomplished many tasks as a result of sleep deprivation. My mindset during those episodes was I might as well be productive while I am still up for the night.

Many individuals who have experienced manic episodes from bipolar disorder do not realize that they are harming their brain cells by trying to "pull an all-nighter." Lack of sleep eventually impairs one's brain function. When the function of the brain is compromised, the result can significantly affect the part of the brain that affects mood and behavior.

Now I am no psychiatrist, but I have enough familiarity with the disorder to conclude how lack of adequate rest and sleep will influence one's mood. There is a heightened level of irritability when a depressive person does not obtain quality rest. This explains the moodiness of the individual with the illness.

My initial episodes with the disorder occurred when I was in college. For everyone who has experienced college, it is a well-known fact that the majority of students who attend college have little regard for rest and sleep. Between the deadlines for completing assignments, studying, attending social functions, and maintaining employment for some, sleep can be difficult to come by.

One's brain can become fully overloaded when trying to sustain a busy school and workload. It is because of one's overwhelming workload that sleep should become desired. When it comes to suggesting that a teenager or young adult should acquire proper sleep and rest, the majority of them will not listen.

If I could tell my seventeen to eighteen year old self that sleep is crucial to the sharpness of one's brain, then I would hope that I would not disregard the warning of my mature self. Sometimes it may take an individual experiencing a severe illness or condition in order to put one's health at the forefront. There should be nothing more important to every human living on earth than their health.

Rest and sleep are synonymous to having a well-functioning brain. This is why most individuals who are under the care of a competent psychiatrist are asked about one's sleep patterns. Mental wellness and sharpness can only be obtained when the individual understands the necessity to sleep.

Once an individual with the disorder can incorporate the need for sleep into one's routine, then that individual has a greater chance of recovery. Although rest and sleep is crucial to the individual affected by the illness, too much of it can have an adverse effect. The depressive person must strive to acquire the same amount of daily rest and sleep on a continuous basis.

I have experienced times in coping with bipolar disorder in which I had little to no rest, and also there were times that I had too much sleep and rest. The goal for each bearer of the illness is to obtain just enough sleep that will help the individual function on an adequate level mentally. When the affected individual receives too much sleep within a given night, that individual can also become lethargic.

In my opinion, a specific time for sleep and rest each night will benefit the individual who is trying to combat the mental illness. There is not any individual, whether a bearer or nonbearer of any mental illness, that can function on an optimum level without sufficient rest. The individual who is affected by bipolar disorder requires more rest and sleep compared to other individuals who are not affected.

One reason why proper rest is required for the individual with the disorder is due to the powerful psychotropic medicine that is prescribed. Many of the psychiatric drugs that are prescribed by a psychiatrist will help the depressive person sleep. Hopefully, the psychiatric medicine does not cause the individual to oversleep.

There must be a balance between setting a specific time for sleep and rest and performing various daily activities. Some who are coping with the disorder must continue to work and go to school despite having the severe mental disorder. It can become a struggle for individuals with the illness to obtain a proper night's rest when one has to cope with one's illness while trying to deal with the stresses of school and work.

I must admit that when I had to go to school and work, I did not have a set time for sleep and rest. My sleep and rest was only acquired when I felt the need to have it. This is the wrong attitude and mindset to have when striving to overcome a severe mental condition in which sleep is required to endure and combat it.

As I recall the times in which I did not set a specific time for rest, I am fortunate that I was able to still function mentally on a consistent level. I mentioned previously that a sufficient amount of sleep could become difficult to obtain when one is in the midst of a full schedule. Because of the busyness of one's schedule and coping with a psychiatric illness, it is imperative that one schedules a specific time each night for rest.

If I can offer any advice to an individual who is coping with, or affected by the disorder, I would suggest that one make it a priority to retire to bed at the same time each night. The affected individual will unknowingly help with one's overall attitude and mood with better sleep habits. When a depressive person maintains a proper sleep regimen, that individual can increase their chances of one's mind and brain functioning at its optimum level.

There was a time early in my diagnosis of the disorder that I did not give any credence to the amount of hours that I should sleep. After I would complete my daily routine, there were times that I did not consider resting. Because I was a young adult during the time of my initial diagnosis, I still had the mentality that I was indestructible.

My lifestyle of going to nightclubs and various functions did not change for several years. Although I did not partake in drinking after my diagnosis, I immediately became the designated driver for some of my friends at that time. I can recall leaving the club in the wee hours of the early morning.

As an individual who was living with bipolar disorder, staying up all hours of the night was not ideal. In fact, I was playing an extremely perilous game with my overall mental health and wellness due to lack of sleep. When I would go out with my friends, I would be lucky to acquire four hours of sleep.

I cannot stress enough how crucial it is for those with a severe mental illness such as bipolar disorder to obtain a sufficient amount of rest. The individual with the condition cannot afford to be up all hours of the night. Eventually, living a lifestyle in which rest and sleep are not considered ultimately catches up with the individual.

If an individual who is not affected by a psychological disorder continues to live a lifestyle in which the individual is sleep deprived, I am certain that he or she will be affected mentally at some point. The mind and brain has to have idle time. We do our brains a disservice when we choose not to listen to it.

In one's brain, there is something within it that relays the message that we need rest. It is up to the individual to either listen to it or ignore it. When an individual chooses to ignore the signal in one's brain to rest, the brain can shut off, thus, affecting an individual's cognitive and mental functions.

I compare an individual who refuses to sleep to a car that needs to be serviced. A car that has to be serviced will typically let the driver know by having a particular light or message which comes on while driving. It is to the discretion of the driver to take heed to the message conveyed by the car. If the driver disregards the message that the car needs to be serviced, then the car will eventually shut down.

The recommendation for an adequate amount of sleep for most adults is approximately seven to ten hours. Some say that an individual is sleep deprived when they get less than six hours of sleep. An individual who has bipolar disorder should not entertain prolonged sleep deprivation.

Those who are not affected with the disorder sometimes have a difficult time functioning mentally from lack of sleep. For example, concentration and memory retention could become affected. If nonbearers of the illness are drastically affected by lack of sleep, then what about the individuals who have the disorder? This is why all who are living with the disorder should strive to obtain at least seven hours of sleep each night.

Individuals living with bipolar disorder may not be able to improve due to lack of sleep. I believe that the depressive person's mood will not become elevated by continual sleep deprivation. The affected individual who does not make a commitment to quality sleep and rest might go through life in a cloud of haze.

I can recall a dangerous experience with the disorder in which I was not resting properly. I stayed up for days. Because of my lack of respect for sleep during that time in my life, my mind and brain was overloaded.

When one's brain is clogged and overloaded, there is an increased chance that the individual will experience some form of a mental breakdown. There are some who ignorantly harm themselves by putting their brain in jeopardy in not doing the simplest thing in life which is sleeping. A rested mind and brain is vital in sustaining and maintaining a life of mental wellness.

The initial time that I became familiar with bipolar disorder, I can vividly recall how my brain became affected by it. I was up late one night talking on the phone. My lifestyle at that time was not conducive to quality rest.

While I was on the phone in the midst of an intense conversation, I literally heard a popping in my brain. It was quite frightening to experience a malfunction in one of the most important areas of the body. Although I reiterate that I am no doctor or expert on bipolar disorder or any other type of mental illness, I knew that when I heard the pop in my brain that it would affect and influence my mental health.

In my opinion, this experience with my brain served as a wake-up call to strive to obtain an adequate amount of sleep at night. I am aware that not everyone will experience the same type of cognitive malfunction as a result from lack of proper rest. I hope that my experience, in regard to a lack of sufficient rest, will serve as a caution and warning to those who do not have the need for quality sleep time.

Sadly, in my case, it took a negative experience with my brain to finally become convinced that sleep is definitely needed. Those who are coping with the disorder should avoid doing more harm to one's brain by not resting adequately. The bearers of the illness must be convinced that sleep gives the brain the power to function properly.

My mental health was significantly affected by a lifestyle that was not predicated on sleep and rest. It is extremely dangerous to the mental health of an individual's brain when it is bombarded with clutter. An individual will unload the clutter in one's brain when sleep and rest are acquired.

If an individual with the disorder would like to improve one's brain and mood, then do not disregard sleep. It is essential to living in a positive state of mind. There is not any sustained optimism without making time for rest. I have never seen an individual who is sleep deprived view life optimistically. We are all one sleepless night from having our brain and mental health affected by sleep deprivation.

Anxiety and worry are key contributors to an individual having lack of sleep. In this world and society that is filled with turmoil and chaos, I can understand how someone could experience sleepless nights. It is easy for an individual who does not have a chaotic life to obtain quality rest.

Some who are dealing with the pressure of just living life are not as fortunate as others to have a consistent sleep pattern. This world and society is increasingly becoming more competitive and fast-paced. There are many who are experiencing the pressure to perform on their jobs, as well as school.

When an individual has pressure to fulfill certain standards, then worry and anxiety will commence. For some who are coping with daily pressure from work and school, sleep can sometimes become put on the backburner. The need for an individual to maintain a certain level of consistency in one's daily tasks may hinder and affect the individual's need for a sufficient amount of sleep.

I think of those individuals who are leading major businesses and corporations. Many of these individuals are pressured to perform at an astronomical level. Some might feel the pressure to outperform their competitors.

Because of the competitive nature of these individual's work climate, the desire to become "top dog" is gained at all costs. The casualty in the quest to become number one in one's respective business climate is sleep. This can lead to some who are in need of becoming dominant to have a mental breakdown.

With the constant pressure of some in the business world to maintain a certain status, some will forego a good night's rest in order to outdo one's business foes. In my opinion, some who are in this position will experience having bipolar disorder. It is never a positive circumstance when an individual has prolonged nights of sleep deprivation. I believe that it can become detrimental to one's mental health when lack of sleep, fear, worry, and anxiety are combined.

I understand the mentality of an individual who is overly ambitious. The overly ambitious individual is typically driven to succeed in spite of the damage that this mindset could have on one's overall mental health and wellness. A mentality of work hard and sleep later is not always the right mentality to have.

Each individual who has a position of power and prominence must learn how to obtain quality rest and sleep. The individual in that powerful platform must learn how to cease from the daily grind. There are not too many individuals who are in positions of power who give sleep top priority.

Some who are affluent are more concerned about trying to maintain riches that the need to have a regular sleep time is nonexistent. It is never a positive outcome when an individual chooses the acquirement of wealth and riches over a healthy sleep routine. Sleep and quality rest are more important to one's overall mental health than acquiring the world's riches.

As an individual matures in life, it can become difficult to obtain an adequate amount of sleep. For some mature adults, sleeping more than five to six hours continuously may not become easy to achieve. Those who are mature and have bipolar disorder should make a tremendous effort to acquire a sufficient amount of rest at night.

Previously, I discussed how an individual who is young does not prioritize healthy sleep habits. Many individuals who are young might feel that if they rest, they might miss out on something. Some who are not mature in life take their sleep time for granted.

Bearers of bipolar disorder should relish sleep regardless of what stage in life that one is in. The one thing in life that no one can retract back is sleep. Sure, an individual can strive to catch up on it at a later time, but all that an individual who chooses not to sleep is doing by trying to obtain it later is binge sleeping.

Any type of rest and sleep is good for the brain and body, but I do not suggest that an individual with bipolar disorder or any other psychiatric condition depend on binging their way to sleep. Binge sleeping usually occurs when an individual does not get enough of it.

Those who participate in this type of sleep pattern should not substitute that pattern of sleep for a regular nightly sleep routine.

I understand that there are times in which we sleep more than other times. Though I am not qualified to know all the answers of why we may have times of binge sleeping as opposed to regular sleep, I can only draw my conclusion on the subject of quality rest and sleep from my experience. Hopefully, you the reader could recall some of your experiences with unhealthy sleep patterns that can influence you to make an enormous effort to change those habits.

When I think of binge anything, I think of overcompensation. In regard to sleep, the individual who is binge sleeping might fall into the habit of doing it all the time. I do not see anything wrong with obtaining an excessive amount of sleep from time to time. There may be other contributing factors besides fatigue that will cause someone to sleep excessively.

Sleeping too much can pose just as much as a problem than not sleeping at all. I vividly recall the experience I personally had with excess sleep. During that time in my life, sleep had become my drug of choice.

Although I slept ideally for seven to eight hours at night, in my mind, I wanted more sleep. This is why I am stating that receiving it was like a drug. I completed and performed the daily tasks that I was required to complete within a given day, but I would anticipate the date that I had with the bed and pillow.

It was not fatigue that influenced my anticipation for sleep, but my underlined mood of depression essentially led me into an unhealthy sleep pattern. This is an example of the other type of extreme sleep pattern that an individual experiencing the disorder could encounter. A healthy and ideal sleep pattern should become the goal for all depressive persons whether they are young or mature.

Facing the world as an individual with bipolar disorder can become difficult. The illness is sometimes unpredictable. Anything can trigger either a manic or depressed episode, which could significantly affect the depressive person's sleep habits.

The individual who is affected by the disorder has a greater chance of bringing down stereotypes of the illness with a proper amount of rest. As I previously mentioned, no individual can function in a sluggish state for a substantial amount of time. When an individual is sluggish, it will affect the tired individual, as well as others.

For example, a coworker who is always tired cannot become productive at the job. This particular individual will seek every opportunity to snooze. He or she will ultimately affect job morale if the employer allows laziness and sluggishness to occur.

What will be the excuse of the individual who is sluggish? First of all, the sluggish individual might give a sob story that they had a million things to do and could not rest. In this cruel world, the only thing that matters to many is results. Individuals who are in an authoritative position are not concerned about the amount of sleep and rest of their subordinates.

Their only concern is with meeting deadlines and the productivity of employees for some who are in positions of power. It is quite rare to encounter an employer who is truly concerned about their employee's overall morale and well-being. Individuals living with bipolar disorder must strive to take care of themselves physically and emotionally.

The depressive person takes care of his or herself by having a regular sleep regimen. It is not always up to others to make sure that one is receiving the proper amount of rest. Those who are affected by the illness should aspire to assume responsibility for an adequate amount of nightly sleep.

A goal for many who are coping with the disorder is to become independent and self-sufficient. The bearer of the illness can become just as productive in the workforce and school as an individual who is not affected by it. Having a consistent and proper sleep regimen for the individual with bipolar disorder could serve as a catalyst for prolonged productivity in almost every goal and task.

Whether an individual has a psychological disorder or not, we all have to face the daily rigors of our world and society. Many of us would like to put or best foot forward each passing day. In order to look our best and feel our best, we must aspire to obtain an ideal sleep routine.

Sleep is part of an individual's well-being. With a healthy dose of it, an individual can confidently face the daily grind of the world. It can become the ammunition that one needs in order to become their very best each morning. In order for a depressive individual to become ready for the constant pressure of the world, it is a necessity to maintain and sustain a healthy sleep schedule.

Many of us have experienced what it is like to take medicine. Medicine is supposed to make one feel better when there is some type of pain or discomfort. It typically relieves the symptoms of discomfort when taken properly.

Some may not realize that sleep can also serve as a type of medicine. How many of us have been dog-tired after a full day of activities? Naturally, one will desire to have rest when the day is busy. Sleep becomes so enticing when one is extremely tired.

I can recall how sleep became a natural medicine when I did a plethora of things within a day. There were times in which I was so tired that I exceeded the ideal amount of sleep. After sleeping for numerous hours, I felt alert and refreshed when I woke up the following morning.

Refreshed and alert is how one should feel each new day. The natural medicine of sleep is vital to one's overall health. When an individual acquires a sufficient amount of nightly sleep, there are some maladies that will not become present.

As an individual living with bipolar disorder, I am aware that psychotropic medicine alone will not always alleviate the symptoms of the disorder. The bearer of the illness must do their part to maintain consistency in mental wellness. Besides having an optimistic mindset in spite of having the condition, I believe that the right amount of sleep will contribute and influence a positive attitude.

Medicine can become quite costly. Some medicines are set at astronomical prices. Many depend on these man-made drugs in order to live each day. Now there is not anything wrong with taking prescribed medicine especially if it is essential to one's health.

In regard to sleep, it does not cost a thing. It is something that does not require a monetary fee to do. The only thing that is required is a comfortable bed. Once an individual obtains the adequate amount of nightly rest, the individual has taken their natural medicine for the night.

Individuals who have bipolar disorder must view sleep as an additional remedy in combating the disorder. The depressive person must view the natural process of sleep as an ally. I am aware that some with the condition might find it difficult to adapt this mindset when coping with it.

Sufferers of the illness can have hope that they will improve when sleep is perceived as a natural medicine. If the bearer of the illness commences to incorporate a healthy sleep pattern in one's life, then there is a chance that the symptoms of the illness will subside. For those who are coping with the disorder, sleep should not take the place of taking the prescribed medicine from a viable and licensed psychiatrist.

I am only suggesting that an individual with the condition do not disregard the importance of having a positive mindset in regard to sleep. This mindset is not a cure-all for the disorder, but it can help the depressive individual sustain a positive mood. Sleep is a positive ally for a productive brain.

The bottom line in regard to sleep is that it is one of the determining factors in living a productive life. Of course, God and prayer are the number one factors of a successful life, but an adequate amount of rest is also a crucial factor to success. An individual who is well rested has the advantage over an individual who does not have proper rest.

Those who are coping with bipolar disorder can have a consistent mood and attitude when a healthy and ideal sleep routine is incorporated into one's lifestyle. In my experience with the condition, I have achieved many of my goals because of my commitment to sufficient rest. Since I have developed a consistent sleep routine, I have not had any manic or depressive episodes.

Although I have reiterated all through this chapter that an ideal amount of sleep is beneficial, it does not mean that the depressive person should sleep all day. When an individual sleeps all day, life will surely pass them by. Also, the individual who sleeps throughout the day will typically be awake all night.

This is an example of a poor sleep habit and routine. Some who have experience with newborn babies would prefer that their baby sleep throughout the night. Because most newborns are awake all hours of the night, the parents of newborn babies do not have the luxury of acquiring a great amount of sleep.

Most parents of newborns report to work sluggish due to the nightly cries of their newborn baby. An individual who is living with bipolar disorder must strive to become the antithesis of a newborn. Once the individual with the disorder recognizes how sleeping throughout the day is unproductive and not beneficial to one's life, then a change in the individual's sleep routine is on the horizon.

The bearer of the condition must not become stubborn in regard to having poor sleep habits. There are benefits in acquiring a healthy sleep pattern. One benefit in obtaining an ideal and adequate amount of nightly rest is waking up in the morning with a newly acquired energy.

Another benefit of receiving the proper amount of rest for the individual who is affected by the disorder is an increased chance of gaining mental sharpness. Mental sharpness will not occur when an individual is sluggish and tired. The depressive individual will likely be on the same course of stagnation with the illness when the individual's poor sleep pattern is not addressed.

Individuals living with bipolar disorder can combat the disease when they take the proper measures in becoming mentally whole. Sleeping no less than seven hours and no more than ten hours a night gives the depressive person a chance to have a positive mood each day. No one can give one's best to the world and society while remaining tired and sluggish. Obtaining a healthy amount of sleep will not only improve an individual's brain functions, but it will increase the individual's level of optimism.

CHAPTER 8

You Can Live a Normal Life

The world does not stop just because an individual is diagnosed with bipolar disorder. This is a world in which some will not have any empathy for an individual with a mental illness. I believe the best thing that an individual who is affected by the disorder should do is to strive to live as normal of a life as possible.

An individual with the condition is just as worthy to live a normal life as the next individual. Those who are living with the disorder must strive to adapt a confident mindset. Developing confidence within oneself does not come at the expense of listening to the negative comments of unsupportive people.

There are some who will say that an individual living with mental illness cannot accomplish set goals. I wholeheartedly beg to differ. Having an illness such as bipolar disorder can sometimes become extremely difficult to manage.

If the individual with the illness has the right support system, then there is a plethora of things in life that one can accomplish. It all commences with the thoughts and attitude of the depressive individual. Some who are bearers of the illness may not view themselves as normal.

Just because an individual is diagnosed with a mental illness does not mean the individual cannot perform activities that an individual who does not have the illness can perform. Those who have the disorder should not limit oneself. The world and society might say that the individual with the illness has little to no chance of living a normal life, but I say it is up to the bearer of the illness to prove otherwise.

I am a prime example of an individual with bipolar disorder that is living one's life on their terms. It was not always easy to have a normal life as an individual with the disorder.

There were times that I thought that I could not resume the activities that I loved.

My mindset changed when I made up my mind that I would journey through life without any regrets. I went from an individual with self-pity and lack of activity to an individual who is active again. When I chose to become the author of my life without giving credence to the opinions of others, I commenced to lead a life that I deem as extraordinary normal.

What about you? Are you living a life of normalcy? Do you allow what others tell you about having bipolar disorder influence your image of yourself? One cannot defy the odds of overcoming the illness by not allowing oneself to become proactive in life. The individual who has a defeatist mindset all because of an unfavorable psychological diagnosis is not living a victorious life.

Bipolar disorder should not equate to a life that is consumed with inactivity. The illness will overwhelm the individual who is not taking the initiative in living a normal life. A normal life consists of setting the same goals and doing the same activities in life that a nonbearer of the disorder can perform.

When I was a substitute teacher some years ago, I would end the class by telling the students that they should be respected. All people must demonstrate respect toward their fellow man. Individuals who are living and coping with bipolar disorder should also be treated with dignity and respect.

In the society in which we live, there are some who do not respect individuals with mental illness. The individuals who frown upon those who have a psychological disorder do not realize that mental illness can come upon them or their loved ones without any full warning. I am certain that when or if the individual who looks down upon those who are mentally ill becomes affected by the condition, the individual will soon see for his or herself how respect should be given.

In my opinion, each individual has a story to tell. There is not anyone who can tell another individual's story without walking in that individual's shoes. In regard to an individual having a mental condition, it is unfair to make judgments and assumptions about the depressive person.

We are all just a life experience away from becoming affected by a psychological condition. This is why all individuals who are coping with mental illness should be respected by other individuals who are not affected by it. Because bipolar disorder and other mental illnesses have become more widespread in our world and society, one would think these conditions would become more widely accepted.

Individuals who are living and coping with the disorder are people too. Those who are affected by bipolar disorder or any other type of mental illness also have feelings. Unfortunately, there are some who give more respect to their family pets as opposed to giving respect to the individual who is mentally ill.

I do not see anything wrong with an individual loving one's animals. All animals must also be granted with respect. The issue that I have with some who do not have a mental disorder is that some treat individuals suffering with mental illness with lack of respect and dignity.

Some disregard the feelings of an individual bearing the condition by labeling the depressive person as *insane*. There was a time in our society that an individual who received the insane label could not become a contributing member of society due to this negative stereotype. Once an individual was deemed insane in previous decades sadly for many affected by a mental disorder, there was no coming back from what others viewed as abnormal.

As an individual who has been greatly affected by bipolar disorder, I refused to listen to the disrespectful ignorance of some. I did not allow society to pigeonhole me into accepting the "insane label." Although I had my fair share of challenges with the illness, I ultimately chose to love and respect myself. If an individual coping with the condition does not love and respect oneself, then how can others proceed in respectful treatment?

If one is not careful, life can pass one by. No one should allow an illness such as bipolar disorder to influence one to deviate from one's goals and plans. I truly and wholeheartedly believe that an individual can accomplish just about anything that they put their mind to.

The only way that a bearer of the disorder can be held back from accomplishing one's goals and dreams is by listening to the negative thoughts of oneself. An individual with mental illness must make a decision about whether or not it will have precedence over one's life. When the depressive individual gains confidence in one's talents and abilities, then there is no stopping that individual.

In my opinion, those who are living and coping with bipolar disorder should set the bar high in regard to accomplishing what they set out to do in this life. Today, there are millions that are bearers of some type of psychological disorder that are defying the odds. Some who are living with mental illnesses such as bipolar disorder are our favorite actors and musicians.

Everyone should set a dream and goal for their lives and individuals who have a mental disorder should not be excluded. Most goals and dreams commence with a thought. Many of us do not share the same exact dream of accomplishing set goals.

There are some who have lofty and extravagant dreams, while some individual's dreams are far less extravagant. For example, an individual who is coping with bipolar disorder might not have a lofty dream of becoming a world-famous musician. The individual who is affected by the disorder might have a realistic dream and goal of not becoming institutionalized again.

With the uncertainty and unpredictability of this severe mental disorder, sometimes the goal of not spending time in a psychiatric institution might become difficult for some to attain. If the individual who is coping with the condition must seek additional help by going into a psychiatric institution again, it does not mean that the individual is a failure. Personally, before I set lofty goals in life, I set minute goals.

One of my goals was to never allow myself to set foot into a psychiatric facility. I must admit that initially, I failed to accomplish this goal several times. It took years of therapy and internal insight to finally achieve this personal accomplishment.

Initially, I failed at my personal goal of not becoming institutionalized. My failures did not stop me from reaching my goals. It has now been over ten years since I was a patient at a psychiatric facility.

I must humbly say that I achieved one of my goals thus far. Another goal that I desired to accomplish was the goal of becoming an author. Thanks to the Creator that I was able to acquire these goals that I set for myself. We all have various goals in life that we set out to accomplish. It does not matter how great or small that one's dream and goal is, one must not allow numerous failures in striving to obtain it, deter one from using these failures as a stepping stone. Failures are normal whether one has a mental illness or not because we all go through them.

Have you ever learned something about someone only to treat that individual differently? It is human nature to subconsciously treat an individual differently after becoming aware of a potential life-altering situation or circumstance that may have significantly affected the individual. There are many who might react either positively or negatively when they become aware of someone's dire condition.

I can recall some years ago when I learned that an acquaintance of mine was diagnosed with a life-threatening illness. My first reaction was shock because this particular individual seemed healthy. After my initial shock of learning about the condition of this individual, I commenced to treat this individual with excessive kindness.

Instead of treating the individual normally, I overcompensated in my behavior. This is a typical behavior of many who become aware of receiving news of a condition or illness that could potentially become life-threatening to someone. Some are not subconsciously aware that although an individual with a life-altering illness or condition might appreciate the outpouring of love and kindness. For some who are coping with these severe conditions, the only thing that they might request is being treated normally.

I believe that individuals who are living with and coping with various psychological illnesses such as bipolar disorder would love to be treated like any other individual. The individual who has the disorder will be able to have some sense of normalcy when friends and loved ones do not treat the bearer of the illness any differently. In my opinion, the depressive person has the potential to live a normal life when he or she does not receive any preferable treatment.

I am thankful that my mother never treated me any different after it was revealed to her that I had a psychological condition. She not only treated me the same, but she always held me accountable for my actions and behavior. My mother did not allow herself to have pity on me.

In fact, because she treated me with normalcy in spite of my early challenges and experiences with the disorder, I can honestly say that I am thriving in life because of her normal treatment of me. It is imperative that all who are coping with bipolar disorder or other severe mental illnesses are treated with respect and normalcy. If the depressive individual is not treated as normal as possible, then as a result, abnormal treatment might cause the individual to not have the social skills to thrive in the environment.

What is normal in a world and a society filled with various people? Although each and every one of us is different, there are some experiences in life that we all should experience. For example, we all should experience what it is like to fall in love. It is a normal emotion for all to enjoy.

When an individual is experiencing the challenge of having a mental disorder, it is imperative that those who are in constant contact with the depressive individual learn how to treat the individual with normalcy. It will certainly make a difference. By the depressive individual receiving normal treatment from others, the individual will have a chance to grow and assimilate in society just as well as nondepressive individuals.

There are some individuals who are living and coping with bipolar disorder that hide behind the illness. What I mean by an individual hiding behind the illness is that some use their condition as a clutch. For some, they might use the illness as an excuse when a situation or circumstance is difficult.

The individual who is bearing the disorder might state that they cannot do or achieve a goal or task because they are *bipolar*. It angers and disappoints me when an individual uses their illness to underachieve. A depressive individual can rise above being defeated by the disorder.

Previously I mentioned how my mother did not treat me any different because I had the disorder. In my household, there were not any limitations on what I could achieve in life. Because I was not limited to what I could achieve, I never allowed having bipolar disorder to be used as an excuse to not overachieve.

It can become difficult to overachieve when society and others try to dictate and decide what an individual who has a mental disorder can and cannot do. Those who have mental illness must not listen to the voices of those who do not encourage one to do better. Sadly, there are some who listen to the negativity of others who say that the depressive person is defeated because the individual has a psychological condition.

When I was diagnosed with bipolar disorder in the early 1990s, I did not have an example at that time of individuals who were overcoming the illness. During that time, an individual who was affected by mental illness had little to no chance of having life of normalcy. It was as though an individual who was diagnosed with the disorder could anticipate a life that was deemed doomed.

Many individuals with the condition at that time could not help themselves in using the condition as a means to gain pity from others. As for myself, I was determined not to become a casualty of living a life of excuses for my condition. Sure, there was a time that I had to overcome the grim prognosis of the illness.

My overachieving and optimistic attitude did not happen immediately. Like anything that has the potential to either become life-altering or life-threatening, it takes time to develop a positive outlook. The individual who is living with bipolar disorder must not remain in the state of self-pity.

I believe that the individual who remains in that state will ultimately use their condition as an excuse to underperform in life's challenges and difficulties. It is essentially up to the discretion of the depressive person to decide whether or not the illness will be used as an excuse to wallow in pity or mediocrity in life. Individuals who are using the illness as a crutch must realize that they are only harming oneself in the long run.

An individual with bipolar disorder or any other type of psychological illness is not the condition. These psychological conditions are illnesses that the individual happens to suffer from. The world and society can become cruel to those coping with the illness. Depressive individuals should learn not to hinder oneself with pity and excuses.

We all would like to aspire to have a joyful life. Sometimes the challenges of life can weigh an individual down. Having a psychological disorder can become an obstacle for many.

It is difficult to enjoy life when the individual who is coping with the disorder is in the midst of a manic or depressive episode. Personally, I understand what it is like to not have any hope in life due to this illness. If one is not careful, bipolar disorder can take away one's joy.

This psychological condition can overwhelm and overtake the life of the individual affected, as well as the life of the individual's loved ones. When enduring the disorder, it may seem that happy days are not on the horizon. As an individual who has lived and coped with the illness for approximately thirty years, I have firsthand knowledge about the hardships and difficulties of the illness.

I can recall how I felt when I was hospitalized due to the disorder. Initially, I thought that my life was over because I was hospitalized with a mental condition. After being hospitalized several times, I did not foresee a bright future.

My battle with bipolar disorder was draining the joy of life out of me. At that dark period in my life, I never thought that I could obtain optimism. Optimism can elude those who are in the midst of the condition.

How can an individual who is battling the disorder feel joy when they are experiencing continuous sadness? Some may have brief bouts of sadness in life, but eventually the sadness cloud will eventually subside. For some individuals with bipolar disorder, the clouds of sadness do not disappear. Sometimes receiving good news in life does not make some with the illness feel happy.

In my experience with the condition, there were times that I thought to myself that I would never regain happiness. Happiness in life comes when an individual is happy with the person they see looking back at them in the mirror. Real happiness is not a result of external factors.

The individual who is coping with bipolar disorder should not allow the condition to stop one from enjoying life. I must say that enjoying life really does commence with an individual's mindset. Once the individual can conquer the pessimistic sadness of the illness, then life will become more enjoyable.

What does a depressive individual have to do to enjoy life? One way that the depressive individual can enjoy life is to focus on the positive qualities and attributes within. Another way to enjoy life for the individual affected by bipolar disorder is to consciously surround oneself with those that have a positive mindset. Some do not realize that we feed off the energy and mentality of individuals with whom we spend the most time. Lastly, an individual who is coping with the disorder can enjoy life by learning from the past but not dwelling on it.

One must not become hesitant in having a vision for one's life. Individuals who have a psychological disorder must also have a vision. A depressive individual's vision for their life is vital in overcoming the condition.

My vision for my life after becoming diagnosed with bipolar disorder has not changed much. Initially, I had a minimal vision. When I gained confidence that I could lead a normal life despite having a psychiatric illness, I commenced to have broader visions and goals.

The first vision I had was envisioning a consistent life of mental wellness. It took some time before this vision came into fruition. I must say that everyone has various visions on how one would like their life to unfold.

Many who are coping with bipolar disorder should envision themselves overcoming the illness. If the bearer of the illness does not envision a life of victory over it, then the chances of successfully combating the disease will not occur. An individual living with the disorder must envision oneself becoming well.

Another vision that I had for my life was completing college. I would not have completed college without envisioning myself over-coming bipolar disorder. There was a time in which my vision of overcoming the disorder, as well as completing college looked rather bleak.

It took many years to live a prosperous life in spite of having a mental condition. My suggestion for individuals who are currently in an uphill battle with a psychological illness is to never lose sight of one's vision of overcoming the illness. The depressive individual must never abandon the visions and goals that they set for oneself.

Patience, persistency, and perseverance are the keys to acquiring most visions. In my experience with coping with bipolar disorder, there were visions that only occurred due to having optimism and a persistent mentality. It can become easy to give up on a vision for one's life when the vision does not occur with haste.

Those who are coping with mental illness sometimes do a dis-service to themselves by limiting their visions. I believe that the individual living with mental illness are just as worthy of having a great vision for their lives as those who are not affected by it. Once the individual affected by a psychological disorder can see one's vision completed and into fruition, then he or she will develop more visions that could become acquired through confidence.

All it takes for one vision to happen is the completion of the first vision. When the initial vision occurs, then an individual will develop other ones. This will ultimately have a domino effect on an individual's visual development.

Visions and dreams are not limited to individuals who are deemed *normal* by society's standards. The individual with a psycho-logical disorder should not limit oneself on the amount of dreams and goals that one envisions. A bearer of a psychiatric condition has just as much right to vision how they want to live their life as the next person.

Life's adversities do not change because one is bipolar. The individual must continue to press on in life in spite of difficulties and hardships. Although many of us have varying degrees of problems, everyone will experience it.

In my own life, I have experienced a plethora of adversities. My adversities have sometimes come about due to my own doing. Nevertheless, the adversities did not cease because of my psychological disorder.

For me, it was a struggle to complete college. I must admit that I encountered various adversities before I was able to reach my goal of graduating. My professors and student loans did not have any mercy on me because of my mental illness.

Personally, I have experienced adversities in both my personal and love life. In my personal life, I have experienced great loss. There were friendships that came to an end due to several reasons.

People come and go in and out of our lives for reasons that are beyond our finite human reasoning. In some cases, the ending of a friendship might not end because an individual has a psychological condition. Sometimes a close friend might move miles away, and because of distance, busyness, and other obligations, one could experience adversity in the friendship.

The scenario of a distant friendship or relationship is a normal life experience. An individual who is living and coping with bipolar disorder is no different. As a bearer of the illness, I can personally confirm that my experience with having a distant friendship did not have anything to do with me having a mental condition.

In regard to my love life, there were some adversities in my previous relationships. One adversity that was prevalent within the relationship was lack of trust. When it comes to having trust in a relationship, we all know that it is the key to having a successful relationship.

With trust, a romantic relationship will endure a plethora of hardships and adversities. Those who are coping with a mental condition might also find it difficult to trust the individual with whom they are involved. Mistrust of an individual in a love relationship can plague the majority of couples, which can contribute to adversity.

Individuals who are coping with psychological conditions will likely experience some of the same life adversities as other individuals who will not experience the condition. Depressive individuals will encounter many heartaches and obstacles. It is both inevitable, as well as a normality in life.

Just because an individual has experience with a mental disorder does not mean that the individual is immune to getting one's heart broken. Though a failed relationship can become both difficult to encounter and experience, it is an experience and adversity that is common for all. Adversity in friendships and relationships does not discriminate because of one's psychological disorder.

Those living and coping with bipolar disorder can live normal lives. It commences with the individual who is affected with the illness, accepting and loving oneself. A reliable support system can also contribute to a life of normalcy.

Although I have dealt with the disorder for many years, I somehow managed to accomplish some of the dreams and goals that I set. Sure, I am blessed with at least one person in my support system that will not allow me to have pity due to my illness. Because I do not have a mentality of self-pity, I have been able to overachieve and defy the odds of an individual with a severe mental condition.

In fact, the main reason why I have been able to live a meaningful and successful life is due to my own confidence and positive self-image. The positive self-image that I acquired in life did not come into fruition when I was initially diagnosed. It took many years of self-examination and soul-searching for me to come into the realization that I can lead a normal life.

In my opinion, an individual who is affected with and living with bipolar disorder is only as good as one's thoughts. I am a firm believer in any individual adapting a positive mindset. When an individual who is living with the disorder can develop a healthy and positive self-image, then the disorder will not dominate the individual's mind, which can have a significant effect on one's psyche.

All individuals who are living and breathing can really accomplish many of their desires. Most desires commence within an individual's mind and heart. It is through the heart of an individual when determination and passion develops.

After I was diagnosed with bipolar disorder, I was immediately determined not to allow the illness to have precedence and victory over my life. There were some doctors that never allowed me to forget that I suffered from mental illness. From my perspective, the prognosis of my condition did not have potential for a positive outcome from the psychological analysis of some of these doctors.

The chances that I would live a life of normalcy from the opinion of those psychiatrists were slim. What these physicians did not take into consideration was my drive and determination to prove them wrong. These doctors were extremely influential in my quest to live the most normal and successful life possible.

I am aware that according to the psychiatric community, there is not any cure for bipolar disorder. An individual who is coping with the illness can either allow the illness to ruin one's life, or they can aspire to live in normality by defying the odds. The individual who aspires to combat the disorder must incorporate the life of normalcy as one of their many goals.

I am living proof that the individual living with a psychiatric disorder does not have to relinquish anything that they desire to accomplish. A normal life can be obtained when the bearer of the illness decides not to become defeated by the potential negative outcome of the illness. The life of normalcy begins and ends with the depressive person's development of a positive self-image.

I believe that an individual living with bipolar disorder can have a life of normalcy in spite of what the world and society says. The individual who is coping with the disorder must have a belief in his or herself that the disorder will not defeat them. Also, the bearer of the illness should make it a priority to not allow the negative thoughts that come about in one's mind at times to have a negative influence in one's life.

An individual coping with a severe mental condition must also find it within oneself to become motivated. Becoming motivated can prove difficult for an individual living with mental illness. This is why it is imperative for the depressive person to work on one's whole self and mental wellness.

When an individual who is dealing with having a psychological condition can conquer the difficulties and hardships of the condition, then the individual will feel a sense of accomplishment. It only takes one day of success in overcoming the battle in one's mind to lead to another day of success. Once an individual can accomplish another successful day in the mental battle, then days will turn into weeks, months, and so forth.

Those who are affected by bipolar disorder are not weak. Some individuals in various cultures view an individual coping with mental illness as subservient. There are some who ignorantly think that the individual with a psychological condition does not have the potential to take care of oneself.

Individuals living with bipolar disorder must aspire to set a positive standard for one's life. In order to accomplish a positive standard for the depressive individual's life, the depressive individual has to formulate a mental image of victory over the disorder. I am a firm believer in an individual developing a positive image of oneself through mental imagery.

We all can be who we want to be in this society. To aspire and strive to become an individual with a positive mental image of oneself does not occur instantly. The development of a mental image of positive wellness and wholeness can only become accomplished by adapting the one-day-at-a-time approach.

Whether an individual has mental illness or not, each individual has the common struggle of maintaining and sustaining a positive mental image of oneself. Confidence and a healthy self-esteem is a normal attribute that all aspire to have and obtain. Most struggle with being confident, which commences and develops in one's mind.

A depressive individual can and will have a sense of normalcy in one's life when a healthy amount of confidence is established. The individual who is coping with bipolar disorder does not have to wait for others to define one's life as normal. Each individual living in this society has to find a way to survive.

Individuals coping with the disorder are not immune to the daily grind of life. Although the condition can become difficult to treat at times, it does not mean that the bearer of the condition cannot live normally in society. Due to the increasing pressure and stresses in life, it is not abnormal for an individual to have to encounter having a mental disorder.

CHAPTER 9

A Consistent Life Helps Defy the Odds

An individual who has any type of illness must be monitored. It is imperative that individuals who are affected by bipolar disorder make it their priority to be consistent in keeping doctor's appointments. There are some who are coping with the condition that think that scheduled doctor's visits are unimportant.

In my opinion, the individual who does not take the initiative in keeping up with one's scheduled appointments will have a decreased chance of overcoming the disorder. Personally, I have known some who are living with the condition that do not see any benefit of maintaining scheduled doctor's visit. Individuals who do not consistently visit one's psychiatrist cannot build a relationship with the therapist.

The therapist or psychiatrist can help the depressive individual with the tools to cope with the illness. One cannot learn how to cope with the severe mental condition without the aid of a viable doctor. Also, by keeping the scheduled doctor's visits, the therapist can gain a better understanding of what treatments work for the patient.

In my own experience with the illness, I have learned how vital it is to have consistency in doctor's visits for my overall health and mental wellness. Without maintaining consistency in keeping scheduled appointments, it ultimately conveys a negative message to the doctor. Furthermore, inconsistency in visiting one's doctor or therapist demonstrates a lack of commitment in combating the disorder.

One has little to no chance of defying the odds of overcoming bipolar disorder by ignorantly and naively thinking that one can overcome the condition on one's own. The individual living with the illness must convey one's thoughts to a licensed professional. Those who are closest to the individual coping with the disorder might have limited tools and experience in helping the depressive individual with the mixed emotions of this unpredictable mental illness.

Bearers of psychological conditions such as bipolar disorder must have a doctor or a therapist who will both listen and reveal to the individual how one can cope and deal with the various emotions of the condition. It is extremely rare for an individual living and coping with the illness to not desire to talk to at least one person about what is going on with them, internally. When an individual who is affected by the disorder consistently keeps doctor's visits, that individual will have a professional sounding board for one's emotions and thoughts.

It is quite liberating for an individual to have someone to talk to who will not judge or insert one's opinion. If the depressive person can develop trust in conversing with a doctor, then that individual will anticipate scheduled doctor's appointments. When trust is established, the chances of the individual defying and overcoming the odds of maintaining consistency in mental wellness and wholeness will increase.

Sometimes individuals who suffer from bipolar disorder do not make the wisest decisions. For some with the condition, impulsive behavior can lead to regret. It is imperative that the individual affected by the disorder learn how to tame and control one's impulses.

Erratic behavior can become detrimental to one's process of overcoming the illness. When this behavior is demonstrated, the individual with the condition lessens one's chances of living a life of consistency. Individuals who are coping with the disease are essentially in a no-win situation when impulses are not under control.

I must admit that there was a time in my life that I acted on impulse. Instead of considering the consequences of my unwise decisions, my mindset and attitude was "you only live once." Some who are not affected by bipolar disorder live by this same mantra.

One who is living and coping with this severe psychological disorder cannot afford to live a reckless and irrational life. Unfortunately, some with the condition choose to only listen to their own advice. Listening to the foolish advice of oneself is definitely not a wise decision.

In a previous chapter, I discussed how it is beneficial for an individual who has bipolar disorder or any other type of mental illness to have a reliable support system. A viable support system can influence the depressive individual to act wisely. Without friends and loved ones who will not allow the bearer of the disorder to succumb to the unwise decisions that could become the result of the disorder, the affected individual would be left to one's own negative vices.

Having accountability and transparency in the depressive person's life could yield to the individual making sound decisions in life. When any individual is aware of how accountability is vital to a successful life, that individual will develop a better revelation of the importance of responsibility and consistency. There should not be any excuses for an individual who has the condition to not be held accountable for one's unwise decisions when love and support are at the individual's disposal.

In my battle with the disorder, I was not always accountable for my unwise actions and behavior. There were some actions that I displayed that could have stalled my development of a consistent life. Thankfully, I have been able to sustain the level of consistency in my decision-making by listening to my support system, as well as not putting myself in situations that could influence unwise choices.

If one can come to the realization that one's whole life is the result of both wise and unwise choices and decisions, then one will become more cognizant about how one lives. The decision to be held accountable for one's choices in life can become difficult. Becoming accountable for one's decisions in life could be the difference between the bearer of the illness living either in consistency or inconsistency.

Self-discipline is oftentimes difficult to acquire. The individual who is disciplined will have success in life. It may not be a plethora of monetary success, but it is the type of success that is obtained by having great moral character.

A life of self-discipline for the individual with bipolar disorder is when the individual takes their prescribed medicine honestly. This means that the depressive person does not become careless in taking it. If the medicine is prescribed for a certain time of the day, then that individual must do his or her best to honor that set time.

There are some who are affected by the disorder who have little to no regard for taking the psychotropic medicine on time. These same individuals leave the responsibility in taking the medicine that is prescribed for them to others. When individuals who are bearers of the condition do not accept responsibility in taking the medicine in a timely manner, it immediately demonstrates lack of self-discipline on the bearer's part.

How can an individual who does not take the initiative for their own treatment expect to overcome the disorder by depending on others? There are some individuals who are affected by multiple and other severe illnesses that cannot do for themselves. For other individuals who are personally experiencing a psychological condition and who are capable of taking care of oneself, there is not any excuse. The individual who has difficulty in taking the psychiatric medicine that is prescribed could invest in one simple timeless product.

The simple product with whom I am referring to is an alarm clock. In these modern times, many of the cell phones have alarms. It does not require a plethora of effort to set an alarm on a phone.

Sadly, there are many that are affected by the disorder who will burden others by missing dosage times. This, in turn, will ultimately affect the overall improvement of one's condition. It is true that the individual who has the psychological disorder cannot be forced to take the prescribed medicine, but I am certain that when an individual is motivated and disciplined in taking the medication, it can make a world of difference in the consistency in the individual's attitude and behavior.

In my experience with bipolar disorder, I was not always disciplined in taking the medication on time. During the time that I was sporadic in taking the medicine at a specific time, my condition did not improve. It was not until I decided to seek the self-discipline within myself that my overall countenance commenced to change in regard to my psychological wellness.

Developing self-discipline can lead to consistency over bipolar disorder. Self-discipline in taking medication for the individual who is bipolar can become a difficult and troublesome task. The individual who is bipolar can only have improvement in one's overall mental health when the commitment to sustained mental wellness is obtained through continuous discipline.

After my last hospitalization, which was over ten years ago, I vowed to myself that I would become consistent in life. I would not have been able to defy the odds of overcoming this disorder without giving top priority to my health. The things I did in previous years I knew that I could not do anymore.

For example, the acquaintances and associates that I held company with who lived a promiscuous lifestyle had little regard for their overall health. I came to the realization that I had to cease from hanging out with these particular individuals. In hindsight, I do not know where I would be mentally if I had continued to keep company with individuals who did not desire to live a wholesome life.

Living a life of consistency is difficult in a world that is filled with temptation. Every individual who is living in this sinful world will become tempted by something. It is not a question of if one will become tempted to carry out desires that could pose a risk to one's mental health and well-being. It is a question of when.

An individual who is living and coping with bipolar disorder should not associate with individuals who are highly immoral. I am not suggesting that the individual affected by the disorder seek out friends and associates who are *perfect* because we all know that an individual who is *perfect* do not exist. What I do suggest for the individual who is bipolar is to seek out friendships with those who have a consistent and highly moral character.

The individual who is bipolar is only as good as the company that he or she keeps. This is not to say that all who are living with bipolar disorder will engage in activities that will hinder one's chances of mental wellness. Associating with those who partake in activities that are immoral could potentially influence any individual whether bipolar or not bipolar to engage in practices that can contribute to an individual's chances of a moral decline.

If one's associates are partying and drinking, then it expected that one's associates would also want their associate to participate in those activities. It can become extremely difficult to avoid partaking in such vices that are harmful to one's mental health when there is peer pressure. Some cannot break the strongholds of pressure from friends and associates even with the best intentions.

In regard to one's character, it is imperative that the individual who bears the psychological condition develop a strong one. High moral character can help the individual who is bipolar avoid situations that will become detrimental to the consistency of one's overall mood. The individual who happens to have the bipolar illness has to exhibit a plethora of courage.

In my opinion, it requires a healthy dose of confidence and self-esteem to not become influenced by peers that are not morally sound. It is not wise for an individual who is bipolar to associate with individuals who will allow them to participate in an immoral lifestyle. The company that the individual who is bipolar keeps can either harm or help the individual with a life of consistence.

Due to the unpredictability of bipolar disorder, living a life of consistency can elude the bearer of the disorder. Some who are coping with the illness are not fortunate enough to have stability. The life of some with the condition consists of never-ending pain, torment, and turmoil.

A consistent life may seem out of reach for the individual living with the illness, but I believe that it is attainable. It starts first with the attitude and mindset of the individual who is affected by the disorder. Secondly, the affected individual must develop the faith in his or herself that the condition can become stabilized.

When I was in the midst of experiencing the illness, I could not have imagined how I would defy the odds and live a life of consistency. Because this illness can become triggered by one negative event, usually the illness can be difficult to control. The depressive individual must learn all they can about the disorder in order to live consistently.

I believe that an individual who understands all there is about one's illness can become better equipped to manage it. In my experience with coping with bipolar disorder, I became aware that my lack of sleep was one of the symptoms that contributed to the onset of my condition. After I became aware about how vital sleep is to my mental wellness, I commenced to take drastic measures in obtaining it.

For some with the disorder, the lack of sleep may not be an issue. Some with the disorder could have a significant level of anger and irritability. If the individual with the condition is aware of the triggers of the disorder, then the chances of the individual living a life of consistency will increase.

Although one with bipolar disorder might somehow obtain a consistent life, it does not mean that the individual is suddenly void of issues and problems. The individual who is bipolar should always examine one's feelings. This is why therapy with a trusted professional and a reliable support system are crucial to the consistent wellness of the bearer of the disorder.

One's therapist and those who support the depressive person are typically concerned with the individual's mood and feelings. A therapist that can get the affected individual to learn how to cope with one's feelings of either extreme euphoria or deep sadness has elevated the depressive person's road to consistence and recovery. The goal for both the therapist and the individual coping with the condition should be for the affected individual not to become too high or too low in regard to one's mood.

Previously, I discussed how a one-day-at-a-time approach to life is imperative to the individual who is striving for consistency in one's life. In reality, one's therapist or doctor will not always be present. It is ultimately up to the bearer of the illness to develop and maintain the coping mechanisms that is acquired through extensive sessions with a licensed professional in order to continuously succeed in overcoming the odds of the condition.

A positive outlook on life can help the individual living with the disorder develop long-lasting victory and consistency over it. It is extremely imperative for one coping with the illness to maintain and sustain a positive mindset. Developing optimism in the midst of the various moods that appear as a result of bipolar disorder might seem as though it is far-fetched.

In my experience with the condition, I did not have a guide-book to the development of consistency in life. From my perspective, there were not any examples of individuals with the illness who were defying the odds. I had to look from within to gain victory over a condition that for a significant period of time in my life was defeating me.

As a result of the illness, there was a time that I had to take a step back from plans that I set for my life. When I was dealing with the effects of bipolar disorder, I never thought that I could become motivated to anticipate another day. With the right doctor and medication, I have been able to enjoy a life of consistent living for several years.

Though I have a minimal support system, I believe that my renewed optimism is a result of my strong belief in God. Acknowledging the presence of the Creator and His Son, Jesus Christ, in my life has enabled me to defy the odds of not allowing this severe mental illness to have dominion over my life.

I also believe that experience and maturity has been crucial factors in gaining victory over the battle of my mind. Today, I fill my mind with things that make me happy. The pressure of overcompensating in my mind due to having a psychological condition has ultimately subsided.

Now I can live a life of continuous happiness because I have become aware of what does and does not work for me. In Addition, I have developed a formula on how to limit the stress and the stressors of life. When I made the conscious decision to terminate relationships that could potentially result in stress, I commenced to slowly develop days of stress-free consistence.

If one would converse with individuals who were previously in my life, I am certain that they would not recognize the person that I have become. After becoming diagnosed with bipolar disorder in my late teens, I was just beginning to scratch the surface of life. Consistency and stability were not of importance to me during that time.

In the uncertain times in which we presently live, consistency and stability is not always attainable. Many are electing to succumb to the chaos of society. It is harmful to one's mental health and wellness when consistency and stability are not present.

An individual with mental health issues are at a disadvantage in acquiring and obtaining a successful and stable life. There is always hope that the individual who is affected by bipolar disorder can defy the odds of having the condition by becoming successful mentally. A mind that is stable can become far greater than all the riches in this perishing world.

Every individual who is afflicted with this severe psychological condition should never lose sight of improvement. If you would ask my former and current doctors if I would live a consistent life, I am certain that they would be surprised. My bouts with bipolar disorder were dire.

There were times that I doubted that I could overcome the chaos and confusion in my mind as a result of an episode. It is quite difficult to envision a life of consistency when this illness is getting the best of you. I believe that determination and faith were factors in my consistency in mental wellness.

In a world and society of constant uncertainty and turmoil, it can become difficult to remain both consistent and optimistic. Some who are coping with bipolar disorder might not have the faith within to overcome it. This illness can consume and overwhelm the individual who does not have a positive mindset.

Without a consistent and optimistic attitude, there is not any chance that one's psychological condition will improve. I can honestly attribute my life of continual mental wellness to having the vision of one day defying the odds. Consistency and wellness cannot be acquired by remaining in the same mental state.

One of the keys to consistency and overcoming the odds of this disorder is to never allow the disorder to define you. Just because an individual happens to suffer from a mental condition does not mean that the individual is incapable. In my opinion, individuals who have a psychological condition have as much mental fortitude as others that do not have the condition.

When I allowed others to determine my mental state, I was not thriving mentally. I am not saying that an individual who is diagnosed with bipolar disorder is not *bipolar*. What I am saying is that the individual who happens to have the psychological disorder does not have to live defeated by the opinions of others.

Some who are experiencing the various episodes of this illness might feel like there is not any hope for one's mental health and wholeness. One might envision a time in one's life in which there is a life of consistency and optimism. I am a prime example of an individual who has been able to overcome a severe mental illness with the development of a positive and healthy attitude.

An attitude and mindset that one will overcome the disorder can equate to the bearer of the illness becoming an individual of consistence. The best compliment that anyone can give besides being a loving and caring individual is an individual who lives one's life with the same level of consistency each day. There is not any magic formula or portion that one must have in order to live daily with a positive outlook. It is up to the discretion of each individual coping with the condition to decide whether or not they will live with consistency and optimism on a continuous basis.

Personally, I have been in the company of some with the disorder who are okay with just barely getting by in life. Complacency and not being motivated is the norm for some of these individuals. An individual who is living with bipolar disorder will not enjoy a plethora of consistency in life when one accepts mediocrity.

Unfortunately, the individual who is coping with the disorder cannot be coerced in acquiring self-discipline and motivation. Sure, there are close friends and relatives that could influence the individual affected by the mental condition to strive for more lofty goals in life. The bottom line in regard to a consistent and successful life for the individual who has a mental disorder is to develop both a positive self-image and a healthy self-esteem.

I can recall how I was not motivated to live a consistent life when I was in the midst of a deep depression. During that period of time in my life, it was difficult to have a positive self-image. My desire for consistency in wellness was lacking.

Having a life of continual wellness should become a goal for all individuals who are living with this disorder. There are some who throw in the towel in life because they happen to be diagnosed with a psychiatric illness. With the availability of potent psychotropic medicine and therapy, the individual affected by bipolar disorder can have continuous wellness in one's life.

It really does matter how the depressive individual views his or herself. An individual who has a negative self-image and a lack of healthy confidence will have an increased chance of remaining in the pitfalls of the disorder. This is why it is imperative that the bearer of the condition continue to formulate positive affirmations and thoughts of oneself in one's mind.

Individuals who are coping with bipolar disorder or any other type of mental condition should avoid comparisons to others. We all have varying approaches to life. In this thing called life, what may work for you might not work for the other individual.

When it comes to confidence and a healthy self-esteem, it can become universal. Confidence in oneself can be acquired when the individual with the psychological condition develops consistency and wellness. Some spend a lifetime striving to develop inner confidence that can only be obtained from the individual within.

In my own life, I commenced to develop my character. I made a conscious decision to become truthful to others, as well as to myself. Also, I made a promise to myself that I would always aspire to do my best. After I made this promise over several years ago, I have personally seen my life transformed.

Every individual, regardless if one does or does not have a mental condition, should pose the question to his or herself, "Did I give it my all on this day?" When one can honestly and sincerely say yes to that question, then confidence and consistency can be obtained. One's desire to be and do one's best in life will have a positive influence on one's consistency and mental wholeness.

Patience is vital to a life of consistent wellness. The individual who is affected by the disorder must demonstrate this virtue with oneself. Becoming consistently well does not happen overnight.

It might take the bearer of the disorder several months or even years to learn how to recognize the symptoms and triggers of the condition. The enemy in regard to living in continuous wellness can be that individual's mental outlook. I believe an individual who is coping with bipolar disorder does not have to be ill forever.

If the depressive individual could adapt a warrior's mindset in overcoming and defying the odds of becoming mentally stable, then the chances of stability in mental wellness will definitely occur. The goal for every individual with bipolar disorder or any other type of mental illness should be mental stability. When a depressive individual obtains this goal, others will see the consistency.

An individual who may be currently struggling with one's mental wholeness and wellness must aspire to recover one's mind. Our mind functions at its best when it is void of mental clutter. With the chaos and despair in the current social climate of the world, it can become quite difficult to maintain and sustain stability in a fragile mind.

The individual who has experienced the varying moods of this psychological disorder must rebuild their mind. In my experience with bipolar disorder, I had to do everything in my power to become strong mentally. In order for the bearer of the condition to become strong mentally, that individual must commit to the process.

Yes, there is a process to becoming an individual who is mentally consistent. Previously, I discussed how keeping up with doctor and therapist visits are essential to the affected individual's improvement. Another part of the process of maintaining stability mentally in the mind of an individual living with the illness is through journaling one's thoughts and feelings on paper.

One would be pleasantly surprised how the method of journaling could positively affect the mind of an individual who is coping with the condition. It significantly helps the individual who has the illness not to internalize. When the depressive individual can develop self-expression through journaling, it can do wonders for the individual's mental state.

After journaling for a substantial amount of time, I commenced to understand my inner thoughts and mindset during that period in my life. Daily journal writing can become both empowering and invigorating. No one can argue or have an issue with your own personal thoughts and opinions.

Personal journaling can serve as a refuge and security to the mind of one who is living and coping with a mental condition. Acquiring refuge and security mentally can dramatically and positively affect the mind and brain. The chances of gaining stability and mental consistency are enormously enhanced through these crucial factors.

My life of consistency in the midst of living with bipolar disorder has been the result of clean living. Before I was initially diagnosed with the disorder, I had little to no regard for living a life void of drinking and partying. I ignorantly equated happiness and living the good life with attending the latest social function.

When I was living the partying lifestyle, I was naively unaware that it would contribute to me having a severe mental illness. I am not saying that all who partake in that way of living will happen to acquire a psychiatric disorder, but I am certain that a prolonged partying lifestyle could influence an individual to have psychosis. Those who are partaking in riotous living do not consider how it could take a toll on one's mental state.

In a previous chapter, I discussed how alcohol and other mind-altering drugs affect the core of an individual. An individual who is engaging in a wild lifestyle is not their authentic self. The mind-altering substances are essentially representing the individual who is participating in the usage.

No one can live a life of continual mental wellness apart from clean living. A life of clean living consists of not turning to alcohol or other substances when life becomes chaotic and difficult. It is also a life of wise choices.

Some of those wise choices might include not keeping the company of certain people. Although an individual who once indulged in a lifestyle of partying might have changed his or her ways, the individual's with whom one was once associated with might feel resentful. A friend or associate who is resentful will do all they can to sabotage and threaten one's life of consistency.

I suggest that an individual who is coping and living with bipolar disorder strive to be in the company of individuals who are practicing a clean lifestyle. If the depressive individual can surround oneself with others that are engaging in a lifestyle of cleanliness, it will influence that individual into a life of clean living. After this lifestyle is established by the one who is affected by the disorder, eventually that individual will be on the road to continuous mental stability.

The lifestyle of clean living can become difficult to obtain. We are living in a world and society that rewards those who are not living cleanly. This is why it is imperative that the bearer of the disorder acquires courage and strength from others who have dedicated their lives to a lifestyle that one does not have to become ashamed of.

I believe that an individual who happens to have a mental condition called bipolar disorder can live a life of consistence in mental wellness. A depressive individual cannot obtain mental wellness on a continual basis alone. The individual with the disorder must become fully committed to the journey and process. It all commences with a daily approach to life. When an individual who is living with the condition is committed and motivated to having mental wholeness and wellness consistently, then there is not any doubt that it can be accomplished.

CHAPTER 10

You Are Who You Think You Are

The stigma of having a mental illness can become quite shameful for the individual with the condition. It is easy to lose confidence in oneself when others are defining you as the individual who is *insane*. Let's face it. There is not anyone who desires to have that label from others.

I can recall being stereotyped and labeled by a particular individual years ago. Though I did not have a personal relationship with this individual, it made me feel guilt and shame for having a chemical imbalance. The individual said, "I was crazy" after witnessing a manic episode that I experienced.

This same individual revealed to other individuals who were not aware of my specific illness that I was *insane*. I went to high school with the person that this particular individual was gossiping with. Thankfully, for my sake, the individual with whom I went to high school with vouched for my character.

Personally, it was embarrassing for me when an unfamiliar acquaintance ignorantly thought that they knew me from one experience. My embarrassing experience as a result of my psychological illness could have caused me to retreat inwardly. I felt shame at the time from the individual who said I was *insane* because she shouted this stereotype in a public place.

I must say that I am fortunate that my negative experience from the acquaintance did not alter my faith and belief within myself.

Unfortunately, there is an enormous amount of people who do not have empathy toward an individual who might be having a difficult time mentally. Some who are struggling mentally may never recover one's confidence after becoming labeled and stigmatized.

The bottom line in regard to the opinion of others is that it should not matter to you what others think about you. In the end, one's opinion of oneself is what counts. No one can physically control what is in another individual's mind and heart.

When I was younger, it used to matter to me what others' opinion of me was. Because of the opinion of others, I was reluctant to reveal to some of my peers that I was coping with bipolar disorder. Instead of seeking support from so-called friends and associates during my severe bouts with the illness, there were times in which I chose to cope with the condition in silence.

Today, I am not ashamed of the illness that has been prevalent in my life for approximately thirty years. I have learned to rely on my own self-affirmations to keep me positive. Eventually, I came to the realization that I had to develop sustainable confidence by becoming acquainted with myself. After years of self-examination, I commenced to think of myself as an individual who is kind, honest, and trustworthy. Because I have developed a sense of self that is demonstrated through my inner character, I am the person with whom I think I am.

Self-worth is vital to the individual who is coping with a severe mental condition. Some who are bearers of mental illness allow the opinion of others to define them. An individual who is living with a psychological disorder must find the courage and confidence in loving and honoring oneself.

There are many individuals who deem themselves as "second-class citizens" because some in society do not honor those who are mentally ill. My suggestion to the individual who is having a difficult time with viewing oneself positively is to focus internally on the individual who you want to become. I am not saying that the individual coping with a psychological condition should aspire to become someone else.

What I am suggesting to the individual who has an issue with confidence and self-worth is to project internally how you desire to become perceived by oneself. When one is genuinely happy and satisfied with oneself, it will definitely have an influence in one's self-perception. One has to ultimately come to the realization that besides pleasing God and His Son, Jesus Christ, we have to also please ourselves.

This does not mean that one should please his or herself at the expense of others. Individuals who act in this way are typically self-centered. Although many who are experiencing mental illness typically focus on oneself through sessions with a doctor or therapist, it is imperative that the depressive individual learns how to distinguish between healthy inner confidence and self-centeredness.

An experienced mental health professional can help an individual who is coping with a mental disorder with the development of a positive self-image. The key to a positive self-image is belief. One cannot develop a healthy self-image if one does not see the healthy image in one's mind.

My road toward a healthy and positive self-image commenced when I understood my strengths and weaknesses. After honestly assessing my abilities and limitations, I soon began to internally blossom. It did not affect my self-worth or confidence when others may have had more expertise on another subject matter than I.

It is essential to one's self-worth when belief and confidence in oneself is attained. If one does not recognize the positive qualities that are within, then that individual will think of oneself as unworthy. The individual who has an unworthy concept of his or herself will most likely become void of self-respect.

Bipolar disorder can become a mental condition in which an individual might display uncontrollable behavior. The behavior itself does not always reflect the individual who might be exhibiting it. An individual who is living with the disorder can become a productive citizen of society when that individual does not define oneself by previous behaviors. As a result of my symptoms and triggers of having the mental condition, there were some behaviors, circumstances, and situations that I was not proud to be a part of, but I always knew that

I would overcome my battle with the disorder by envisioning and thinking of myself as mentally whole and well.

Because I have managed to develop a positive self-makeup of myself, I have been able to sustain mental wellness. Honestly, I do not think of my illness on a daily basis. I live life each day with contentment and joy.

I believe that my faith and belief that I could defy the odds and overcome bipolar disorder has contributed to a positive self-image. It has been difficult at various points in my life to think that I could ever become whole mentally. There have been times in which I thought that this condition would always have power over me.

Now I can recall how I gave this illness dominion simply by the way that I thought internally. One's thoughts are manifested by one's behavior. We tend to act out our thoughts by our actions.

If an individual is content and happy with oneself, then that individual will become a joyous individual. For many who are struggling with bipolar disorder, it is a mental illness that can steal one's joy and happiness. The condition can bring sorrow, regret, and shame to both the individual coping with the condition, as well as those closest to the bearer.

When the bearer of the illness can think of his or herself as mentally stable and whole, it will have a positive effect on the bearer's relationship with others. For example, an individual who thinks of oneself as stable will tend to demonstrate behaviors that are consistent with rationality. An individual who is reasonable in their thinking can and will become a more pleasant person for others to be in the company of.

The only way that an individual who is living and coping with bipolar disorder can defy the odds of the disease and improve is by how one views oneself. If one is defeated and overwhelmed by this illness, then that individual will have a decreased chance of self-assurance. Sometimes the compliments and pleasantry of others will not be enough for an individual who is having a difficult time with their self-makeup.

For the individual who is struggling internally, the only way that the individual can receive and enjoy a compliment from others is by developing a positive self-image of oneself. In my own battle with the condition, there were times that others' compliments did not have a long-lasting effect on me one way or another. After I commenced to think of myself as a worthy individual of character, I was able to view myself in that way.

One must not seek externally when aspiring to become mentally whole. This is an error that many commit who are striving to understand who they are internally. Some, desiring to become victorious in the mental battle over one's mind, must focus on winning the battle over the disorder that commences and ends from the mind within.

In this world and society in which external stimulation is a factor in many facets, it is easy to disregard how an individual should give one's internal makeup top priority. If the individual thinks of his or herself positively despite having a severe mental disorder, then that individual will thrive and overcome the odds just by one's thoughts.

Overcoming a severe mental illness such as bipolar disorder can become difficult to accomplish. This illness cannot be overcome by having a negative self-perception. A positive self-perception of oneself could make a world of difference in combating the condition.

I am aware that it is not easy to have a positive perception of oneself when the disorder is overtaking one's mind and emotions. In addition, I believe that the individual who overcomes and defies the odds of having a prominent mental condition should not become accepting of what doctors, loved ones, and close friends tell one about the limitations of having the disorder. If the individual with the condition can disregard what others say about what the depressive individual can and cannot accomplish in life, I am certain that the bearer of the illness will become a certified over comer and overachiever.

My experiences with bipolar disorder were definitely difficult to overcome. I can recall a time when I was in a dark place because of the illness. There was a particular time in which I was so depressed that I retreated for days in a darkened bedroom.

Those who cannot relate to being deeply depressed are not aware of the challenges of completing daily tasks that may seem unimportant because it is routine. When I was in that deep, depressive, and darkened state, it was difficult to love myself. Every flaw and shortcoming that I saw within myself was significantly magnified as a result of my battle with bipolar disorder.

In 2010, I had enough of this severe mental illness continuously having precedence over my life. It was in the summer of that year that I willfully decided to take my life back. I was through experiencing the roller coaster of emotions of this illness.

Due to my unpredictable moods as a result of the disorder, I lost a plethora of meaningful relationships. My romantic relationships with former girlfriends were casualties from my own irritable and sometimes erratic behavior. It was through intensive self-examination and reflection that I discovered that bipolar disorder was ruining the relationships that were dear to me.

Previously, I mentioned how the individual with the disorder might not have control over one's mind and behavior. When this occurs, strange and eccentric behavior will occur. The individual who is experiencing the mental battle from within may not realize how much of a strain that the disorder can put on personal relationships.

Simply put, it takes a plethora of love, understanding, and patience to be in a romantic relationship with an individual who might be having a difficult time with one's emotions and feelings. Some who are living and coping with the disorder might find it excruciating painful to express one's thoughts. For some who are affected by the condition, an intense romantic relationship could trigger painful emotions, which could become detrimental to both the depressive person and the other partner in the relationship. An individual can defy the odds in having a viable, reliable, and meaningful romantic relationship when the depressive individual can master one's mind and thoughts, thus, leading to self-control.

God can do the unimaginable. I believe that I have overcome and defied the odds of having a severe mental condition because of my belief in Him and His Son, Jesus Christ. Before I was initially diagnosed with bipolar disorder, I did not have an allegiance to the Almighty.

I am not saying that I was an atheist because I was always aware that the heavenly Father existed. In my opinion, the Creator had to allow me to go through the pain, guilt, and disappointment of having a severe mental illness in order to turn to and live for Him. My journey into mental wellness and wholeness was never easy.

There was a time in which I thought to myself, *Why me?* Now my thoughts are, *Why not me?* I am a firm believer that everything in life happens for the heavenly Father's divine purpose. It is humanly impossible for me to figure out the main reason why I experienced this illness.

Yes, I am talking in the past tense. If an individual with whom I met years ago would have known the individual whom I have become today, I can confidently say that I would be unrecognizable. The goal for every living and breathing person walking on this earth is to mature.

Bipolar disorder, because it is a mental condition of extreme highs and extreme lows, if left unchecked, it will not allow the individual who is affected by the disorder to become content and grow in life. No individual who has experienced the disorder can overcome it without spiritual assistance and a reliable support system. This particular illness requires courage and strength in becoming victorious over it.

The only way that an individual can conquer anything in this life is by having and maintaining a right relationship with God. Mental disorders are not from the heavenly Creator. It is a result of living in a chaotic world, which can weigh heavily on an individual's mind.

I can recall my state of mind when I was initially diagnosed with the illness. My mindset during that time was filled with anxiety, confusion, guilt, shame, worry, and fear. Because I experienced these emotions in my heart and mind for a substantial amount of time, my mind commenced to become bombarded and overwhelmed by the negative emotions, thus, resulting in a mental breakdown.

It can become a frightening feeling when an individual loses control of one's mind. Unfortunately, some are not fortunate to ever regain it back. For others who are living with and coping with the disorder, it may take a plethora of time to regain control of a mind that might be overwhelmed with thoughts of confusion and chaos.

An individual who is having a difficult time with their mental stability must not lose sight of one's hope. With the assistance of God, loved ones, and a doctor or therapist with the best interest of the depressive individual, the individual can land on the right side of one's mental health.

Sufferers of bipolar disorder must strive to overcome the outside factors that can contribute to either a manic or depressive episode. As I am writing this book, there is a deadly pandemic that is wreaking havoc called coronavirus or COVID-19. It can become difficult to maintain and sustain one's mental wellness when many around the world are losing their lives.

It is not always easy to sustain one's mental health in the midst of peril. My suggestion to anyone who is having a difficult time mentally is to pray. One cannot go wrong with praying to the God of comfort.

I believe that an individual can still defy the odds and overcome this disorder while in the midst of a worldwide crisis. The individual who is affected by a psychological disorder must realize that one day, there will not be any more sickness. In this life, sickness is temporary.

When I adapted the mindset that sickness is temporal, I was able to embrace having a mental illness. Illnesses are a part of everyday life. Many will experience some form of an illness or condition in this lifetime.

Although some who are in the psychiatric community of doctors, nurses, and therapists might not offer hope in acquiring mental stability from having a mental disorder, I believe that an individual can overcome the disorder by becoming both realistic and optimistic. No one can overcome any illness whether psychological or nonpsychological through self-denial. The first step in overcoming any type of illness is acknowledgment. One must accept the fact that they have a condition.

The sooner that the individual with the illness accepts their diagnosis, the more proactive the individual can become. In regard to an individual living and coping with a condition such as bipolar disorder, a realistic attitude could prove beneficial. Individuals with a realistic and proactive approach toward the disorder will most likely become more aggressive in combating it.

Taking an aggressive approach in overcoming this condition entails taking care and loving oneself. It requires the depressive individual to develop an unshakable and consistent positive self-image that can weather any storm. After the development of an unbreakable positive self-image is obtained, then there is not anything that an individual with a positive mindset cannot achieve.

Next to the heart, the mind is extremely vital and imperative. The mind is the epicenter of how one views his or herself. Once a positive and optimistic mindset is established, it will greatly enhance an individual who is coping with mental health issues chances of obtaining a positive mental makeup, as well as greater odds of mental wellness.

If an individual with the disorder acquires mental wholeness, then that individual will gain mental stabilization. Mental stabilization comes into fruition by therapy, medication management, and a positive self-image. In a world of turmoil and confusion, a positive self-image can combat all of the negativity that might surround us.

Sadly, some who are coping with bipolar disorder do not appreciate their own self-worth. If an individual who is living with the disorder desires to defy the odds in overcoming the condition, the individual must work on not being as sensitive to others' opinion of them. The bearer of the illness can overcome the condition by not focusing on the negative labels and stereotypes that society places on them.

It is beneficial to the depressive individual to surround oneself with positive people. No one can combat and overcome the illness with a cloud of negative attitudes from the individuals whom one is closest to. In this age of pandemics and modern technology, distance from friends and loved ones are increasingly becoming the norm.

I understand the challenges that an individual who is living and coping with this psychological condition could encounter. One challenge that the society of today poses for any individual whether one does or does not have a mental illness is isolation. When an individual is lonely, that individual is most susceptible to enduring an episode.

Now there is something called physical distancing that has resulted due to the COVID-19. Millions in this country and all around the world have been forced to participate in the isolation from others due to fear of catching this invisible and mysterious virus. Because of the threat of catching the virus, which can become transmitted through minimal human contact, it is now unsafe to give friends and loved ones a simple act of affection such as a hug.

We all need some form of love and affection especially those individuals who are combating severe mental illnesses. What one thinks of in regard to his or herself in one's mind is now important as ever. This is why it is imperative for the individual who is battling the disease to somehow find it within oneself to unconditionally love the person who reflects back at them in the mirror.

Only a relationship with the Creator and His Son can help the individual who is struggling with a psychological disorder to love oneself and overcome the odds of allowing an illness like bipolar disorder to defeat them. I believe that the support of at least one supportive friend or loved one can help an individual who is clinically diagnosed as bipolar to have mental stability in the midst of a world becoming increasingly more uncertain and unstable. The environment and world can become unstable, but the individual who is coping with bipolar disorder must realize that they are ultimately the captain of one's own mind and thoughts.

Though one might be diagnosed with the disorder, it does not mean that it defines who the individual whom is affected by the condition really is. One is only defined by the individual's own mental image. Although we live in a world and society that is made up of various opinions, the self-opinion of oneself is what ultimately matters. Yes, your self-opinion and synopsis of yourself is the difference between overcoming the odds of mental wholeness or being at the mercy of an illness that is predicated on thoughts of sadness, anxiety, and thoughts of confusion.

With the new normal of physical distancing and isolation, it is more imperative that an individual who is living with bipolar disorder views his or herself positively. I cannot stress enough how vital it is to have positive affirmations. An individual who is coping with the disorder must focus on one's positive qualities in order to combat and overcome an illness that can have dominion over one's mind and thoughts.

A depressive individual in these uncertain times cannot depend on external factors to help one to overcome the condition. If the individual who is coping with the illness cannot find at least three or more positive qualities about oneself, then that individual is not looking hard enough from within. Every human that is fortunate to be a member of this world and society has qualities within oneself that one can focus on.

Fear, worry, and anxiety can become difficult to eliminate in the world in which we live. If an individual who is struggling with the disorder can turn their attention to a loving God, then it will make a world of difference in one's thoughts and feelings. When an individual can view oneself as a child of God, then I am certain that an individual who views his or herself in that way can overcome just about any affliction.

In my experience with bipolar disorder, it was a struggle initially to have positive thoughts toward myself. There were times in which I thought that I would never regain the confidence that I had before my diagnosis. Because I was diagnosed with a mental illness, there was a period in my life that I thought of myself as inferior.

This negative view of myself commenced to subside when I became a true believer in God and Christ. Although doctors are beneficial in the treatment of many illnesses and sicknesses, they cannot replace the hand of God in one's life. As an individual who has experienced the various moods and extremes of bipolar disorder, I am the unlikeliest person to state that I have overcome the condition.

Do not get me wrong, I am unqualified to state that I am completely cured of the illness because I am not a doctor or a therapist. I am just an individual who has experienced the various peaks and valleys of a severe psychological disorder that could become deadly if left untreated. Also, as a bearer of the illness, I have been fortunate enough to only have one negative experience with entertaining the act of suicide.

Our heavenly Father, as well as His Son, Jesus Christ, desires that all who believe in them do not give up on life. Bipolar disorder is a disorder that can lead someone into deep thoughts of sadness and despair. It is difficult to climb out of that mental state without surrendering one's whole mind to the Creator who created you.

It does not matter how anyone may perceive you because you are God's child. He does not turn His back on those who humbly, honestly, and diligently seek Him. Man might say one thing, but only God can help someone truly overcome a psychological disorder that can influence someone to have a negative self-image and perception of oneself.

I have been able to defy the odds of living with bipolar disorder for these past several years because of my positive self-image and mindset. The positive image and mindset that I developed has been the result of years of positive thoughts. Now I do not focus on the flaws and shortcomings that I have.

Another reason I have been able to overcome this disorder is by maintaining a consistent prayer and spiritual life. There is not any way that I could have sustained years of mental wellness and wholeness without it. Also, I have learned how to have self-acceptance toward myself.

Self-acceptance is vital if the individual who is affected by the disorder plans to combat the disorder on a continual basis. It may take a plethora of time for one to develop self-acceptance in a world and society that is image conscious. When an individual can develop self-acceptance, then self-love is on the horizon.

An individual who has genuine self-love toward oneself will think that one is an individual worthy of a joyous life. After joy is established in one's life, there will not be any room for deep sadness and self-loathing. It will require a combination of meaningful activities in order for the depressive individual to think of oneself as joyous.

First of all, it is difficult to acquire joy in the midst of these uncertain times. True joy is different from happiness because true joy can be sustained through various trials and circumstances. Happiness, on the other hand, can sometimes waver. It is not as consistent as joy.

Bipolar disorder is a mental illness that does not equate to joy for the individual with the condition. The end result of the condition typically results in confusion and inconsistent thoughts. Due to these thoughts, it will cause the bearer of the illness to have doubt.

Once someone has doubt in one's life, that individual will tend to not think of oneself as an individual with confidence. My suggestion for the individual who is coping with feelings of doubt is to focus on the heavenly Creator and His Son who can erase those thoughts and feelings of uncertainty.

This disorder will have the individual who is affected by it question one's thoughts of doubt regularly. Those who have these thoughts are not living joyously. Instead, these individuals are ultimately living in a psychological nightmare.

In my experience with bipolar disorder, I experienced years of self-doubt, which contributed to poor self-imagery. There were times in which I thought that I could not accomplish what I set out to do because of my feelings of doubt and inadequacy due to this psychological disorder. When I made up in my mind that I was a capable individual, the symptoms and triggers of this mental illness did not have any bearing on what I mentally thought toward myself. I have been able to have joy from within because I am content with the person with whom I have become.

Defying and overcoming a severe mental illness such as bipolar disorder can be accomplished. Regaining confidence despite having the condition could become difficult to obtain, but it is possible. It all depends on how the individual with the disorder views one's circumstance and predicament.

With the increasing diagnosis of millions with the disorder, an individual who is diagnosed does not have to wallow in guilt, embarrassment, self-pity, or shame. No one is immune to acquiring a mental condition. Though the mind is powerful, it can become fragile when overloaded.

This book was intended to give hope to all who are affected and experiencing bipolar disorder. Those who are coping with the illness can live normal and outstanding lives. The depressive individual can be prosperous and victorious in life by sustaining and maintaining long-lasting mental wellness. In spite of external confusion and chaos, which are plaguing our present world and society, the individual who is bearing the illness can become mentally stable.

A healthy mind is the goal for every individual who is living and coping with bipolar disorder. If the bearer of the disorder could develop a good patient to client relationship with one's psychiatrist or therapist, then that individual has a greater chance of one's mind functioning mentally with consistence. This can also be obtained when the depressive individual does his or her part in the process.

The individual who can defy the odds on the journey to mental wellness and wholeness must faithfully take the required dosage of medicine that is prescribed by a licensed psychiatrist. There must be a level of consistency in taking the prescribed medicine by the individual who is living and coping with the disorder. In addition, a consistent sleep and exercise routine could affect the individual with the disorder by resulting in a positive mood.

In maintaining these regular routine regimens, the depressive individual's mood has a chance of becoming leveled, but this process requires discipline and determination. Once the individual's mood is leveled, then he or she is a candidate for overcoming the odds of not succumbing to the disorder. When one can accumulate more good days than bad days in regard to one's mood, then that individual is on the road to recovery and defying the odds.

Our current world and environment can lead anyone to have an encounter with mental illness. Prayer, reading, and meditating on the Word of God can also help with an individual's anxiety and mood. In my journey to mental wholeness and wellness, the Bible has been one of the key factors for me in the development of consistency in mental wellness for over ten-plus years.

If you or your loved ones are having a difficult experience with bipolar disorder, I suggest that neither one of you lose your hope and patience. With the support of one's family, loved ones, doctor, and therapist, an individual can defy the odds and overcome bipolar disorder if one never loses sight of one's vision and goal of becoming whole mentally. As I conclude this book, I would like to inform you, the reader, that I am an individual who has defied the odds in overcoming the battle over bipolar disorder.

ABOUT THE AUTHOR

Romain U. DuFour, III is the author of the book, *The Winning Christian*. He is a graduate of the University of Houston-Downtown with a bachelor's degree in psychology. DuFour III writes in order to help those in need of hope and encouragement. It is his goal to spread a message of love and compassion toward others in a dreadful time in human existence.

CPSIA information can be obtained
at www.ICGtesting.com
Printed in the USA
LVHW090935210221
679536LV00025B/477